# MR. DARCY'S SEASIDE ROMANCE

## ALL GO TO BRIGHTON! A PRIDE AND PREJUDICE VARIATION.

## VIOLET KING

PEMBERLEY PLAYGROUND PRESS

**After Mr. Darcy's disastrous proposal at Rosings, will Brighton offer a second chance?**

Safeguarding Lydia's virtue is no easy task. Not with Lydia throwing herself into trouble at every opportunity. The flirting. The gambling hell. Mr. Wickham! And when Mr. Darcy arrives in Brighton, Lydia's virtue is not the only thing at stake. Can Elizabeth save her sister without risking her heart?

Hiding the betrayal of a friend is no easy task. Especially not when Mr. Bingley drags Mr. Darcy to Brighton before Darcy can verify the truth of Miss Jane Bennet's continuing affection. Add Wickham, smugglers, and Miss Elizabeth Bennet to the mix, and friendship is not the only thing at stake. Can Darcy prove himself worthy of a second chance before Elizabeth breaks his heart again?

Find out in Mr. Darcy's Seaside Romance, a new addition to the Jane Austen Challenge: All Go to Brighton Project! Mr. Darcy's Seaside Romance is a sweet novel of 53,000 words with a touch of danger and a healthy dash of romance, all sealed with a kiss.

This book is a part of the "Jane Austen Challenge: All Go To Brighton" project (JaneAusten-Challenge.com). The Jane Austen Challenge asks authors of Jane Austen inspired romances to write a book of any length which includes a featured plot point in their story. For this one, the inaugural, it's Brighton!

DEDICATION

First I give thanks to God and my mom for supporting me even on my grumpiest writing days. Next, a HUGE THANK YOU to Elizabeth Ann West who encouraged me to try my hand at writing in the world of Pride and Prejudice. Also, so much love and gratitude to the whole writing productivity gang, including Pat, Mr. Sparkle, Susannah, Dana, Cora, Echo, and my admin wench, Bella who kept me getting those words on the page with gold stars galore!

I am also thankful to the wonderful readers and reviewers on FFnet, including but not limited to Regency1914, NotACursedChild, Dw.618, Gaskellian, MerytonMiss, EightYearsandaHalf, Twilight Reader Too, Liysyl, Wermeth, Lynned13, English-

LitLover, and countless others who encouraged me and let me know when my Regency (and overall story) went awry, you have my heartfelt gratitude.

And **I am wildly grateful to my ARC team** who have generously read this book in advance and given their honest reviews of my work. You are all angels in human form!

Lastly, super grateful to have had the chance to participate in the Jane Austen Challenge (janeaustenchallenge.com)! What a wonderful group of writers!

Thank you all!

# INTRODUCTION

Did you know men and women in the Regency era often swam nude? I was surprised to learn this too, but this is one of the reasons why the beaches at Brighton are separated by gender. You can learn more about this and see some etchings from the time of ladies bathing in the nude here: https://kathleenbaldwin.com/ladies-swim-regency-era/

Swimming in bathing gowns, which were basically full coverage, relatively lightweight dresses, was also common. Though as you will learn in this book, they do make swimming more troublesome.

Also, **keep your eyes peeled for Ernest the seal**. There's a deeper story there, and one you'll see throughout all of the Jane Austen Challenge: All Go To Brighton books.

# CHAPTER 1

"Lizzy, you have convinced me." Mr. Bennet stood, his lips tight with the corners turned downwards with an uncharacteristic frown. "If our Lydia is incapable of weathering the perils of Brighton on her own, then you, being possessed of a keen sense and an agile mind, must accompany her."

"Papa!" Though Elizabeth could not deny she felt some small temptation to visit the seaside, she could imagine no greater difficulty than being forced for weeks to rein in her younger sister's high spirits, especially when Lydia faced the twin temptations of male attention and the opportunity to flirt as much as she wished. "It is not seemly. I cannot force myself, uninvited, into Mrs. Forster's home.

While I accept my bonds of familial loyalty, it is well acknowledged that Lydia and I share no special closeness. I will be an imposition. Papa, do not ask this of me," Elizabeth pleaded.

"I know this is a burden, but if Lydia's summer in Brighton is as dangerous to her character and reputation as you have so passionately argued, then I have little choice but to insist you accompany Lydia to ensure both her appearance and substance of virtue."

Pulling at her skirts and gripping them in tight fists, Elizabeth attempted to clarify her original point. "I am not asking, even if they had invited me, to summer in Brighton. I am saying I do not wish Lydia led astray. Forbid her to go. I cannot ask it more plainly."

"Lydia is indeed a silly girl, but it is also because she is, here, a large fish in a tiny pond. In Brighton, her youth and vivacity will not be so different from that of other young ladies, and under your watchful gaze, I suspect any temptations shall be circumvented. She may go, but only if you accompany her. As much as it pains me to lose your intelligent conversation for a time, what must be must be."

Elizabeth recognized from the stubborn tilt of her father's chin and the hardness in his gaze, she could not change his decision and so took her leave. Heart heavy and chest tightening in a manner reminiscent of one of Mrs. Bennet's spells, Elizabeth could but pray her presence would be too much of an imposition for Mrs. Forster to receive them both.

Only then would Lydia and Elizabeth be saved.

# CHAPTER 2

"Louisa must be exaggerating." Bingley's attempt at cheer fell short at his eyes. "You are certain you remember nothing of Mr. Dunham?"

Darcy shrugged. "He was three years my junior." The boy had been fair and possessed of a good allowance, enough to supplement the house meals. He had also been fond of sweets, Darcy remembered vaguely. And ostentatious, the sort of boy who would do anything to impress others with his wealth and bravery.

Bingley and Darcy sat across from each other in his carriage. Bingley, not a reader, attempted, with limited success, a game of Patience on a tray upon his lap.

Darcy, not one for cards and having no attention for his correspondence sent forward from Pemberley, held an open letter in his lap while his gaze traced the passing landscape.

Bingley forced a smile. "Louisa has always been a bit high-strung when it comes to her sister. If Caroline were to fall in love, she would do so carefully, and with someone wholly appropriate. When we arrive, we will find Caroline has the situation well in hand. Then, we shall bathe in the sea and entertain ourselves with cards and dancing."

"I am not one for dancing."

Bingley chuckled. At least that was genuine.

For most, a trip to Brighton was a holiday. For Bingley, whose sister might be engaged in an unfortunate courtship, it was an issue of fraternal pride and duty.

For Darcy, the journey was a reminder of his failures and possibly an attempt at redemption.

Darcy's secret rested like a hot worm in his guts. Miss Elizabeth's revelations of her sister's affection for Bingley had seemed genuine. The woman had certainly spared no thought for impressing or pleasing Darcy. She had met his every approach with fire, and though her judgment of him and Wickham, the cad, could not be farther from the truth, Darcy did not doubt the sincerity of her emotions. This meant Miss Elizabeth at least believed in her sister's affection for his friend.

Whether Miss Elizabeth was correct was another matter.

If Bingley, still trusting in his friend's judgment, had not begged Darcy to come and reacquaint himself with his schoolmate, Darcy's would not have gone to Brighton. But, whether Bingley knew it, Darcy recognized the debt between them. He had wronged his friend, and he had no true way to mitigate the offense.

To determine if Miss Bennet's affections were still true to Bingley, Darcy would have to return to Longbourn and speak with the young woman. Worse, he would have to face Miss Elizabeth, who had so thoroughly unmanned him in the projection of his proposal.

Blast her! Blast her observations and her unwillingness to accept his affection. Perhaps, he was willing to admit, at least to himself, he may have been in the wrong to express his opinion of her family as a part of his proposal. Though Miss Elizabeth, being imbued with a higher gentility, ought to have recognized the compliment he paid her in the comparison.

Darcy was considered a fine catch to other women of his acquaintance. Miss Caroline Bingley had practically thrown herself at him given the least provocation.

This made Miss Bingley's sudden courtship with another unsettling, even as Darcy had no interest in marrying the woman himself.

How had Darcy gone from being admired to reviled and then ignored in a span of weeks?

Or perhaps, he had never been admired for himself. Perhaps it had always been his 10,000 a year and extensive lands.

A humbling thought.

Worse, he could not put Miss Elizabeth Bennet from his mind. Perhaps because her interest in him, or lack of it, had nothing to do with his 10,000 a year or property.

Has Miss Elizabeth read his letter? It had been improper to write to her directly, and yet, how else could he explain the error in her judgment and, humiliatingly, the error in his own?

"Darcy, are you well?" Bingley said, looking up from his cards.

"Very well."

"I had thought you disinterested in my sister.

The thought of her marrying another man cannot—"

"No. I am not thinking of your sister."

Bingley raised an eyebrow. "Then who are you thinking of?"

"No one."

Bingley laughed. "Yours is not an expression one wears when thinking of 'no one'. I know. I have seen it in my own reflection enough these past months." Bingley's voice softened. "Someone has broken your heart, have they not?"

Darcy's first instinct was to reject his friend's words. Yes, he had proposed to Miss Elizabeth, and yes, she had taken every effort to stomp his heart into dust, but had she succeeded? No. He would not give her the satisfaction.

Best to put Miss Elizabeth Bennet from his mind. Darcy was here to help his friend, whose sister might be taking an unfortunate path. He said, "I have not spoken with Mr. Dunham since we were in public school.

Darcy tried his best to remember the younger man. "His father gave Phillip a healthy allowance, and he spent it. At first on fine foods, and later on women. But none of this is unusual for a young man, and I had always felt him more interested in impressing others than vice for its own sake." As Darcy spoke, the young man grew clearer in his mind: large boned and stocky with a small but noticeable rounding of his gut. "If Mr. Dunham is still pursuing such interests, Miss Bingley will set her attention on more suitable prospects," Darcy mused.

Bingley nodded, but his lips were pressed together. He tapped his finger against his cheek and said, "Perhaps if Mr. Dunham were an ordinary man. But he will inherit a title, and my sister has always been enamored of titles. Caroline and Louisa were treated terribly by the other girls at the seminary school my father sent them to when they were younger because our money comes from trade."

Darcy, who had been sent away for three years to Eton, knew how difficult other children could be. As the nephew of an Earl and a significant fortune forthcoming, Darcy had avoided the brunt of the other boy's hazing. But for those without his bona fides, boys with parents in trade and the occasional child sponsored by a lord or lady as a charitable expense, had faced brutality. Children were vicious monsters much of the time. Bingley, having also boarded at Harrow, had somehow avoided the brunt of it, due to his unusually pleasant nature and a fine right hook.

Darcy nodded. He asked, "If you do not approve the match, will Miss Bingley...?"

"I had not imagined myself in a position to exercise better judgment than Caroline." Bingley scrubbed a hand through his hair. "I may be the heir, but Caroline, as often as not, is the master of our affairs. She manages our household with an iron fist, and, our solicitor and steward are terrified of her. Once, I remarked Caroline may have better been born the son and I the daughter, and she laughed and said the other ladies would eat me alive."

Darcy wondered if he would have had a better impression of Miss Bingley if he had met the sister his friend spoke of so fondly. But even when he spent weeks at their home, Caroline was always the perfectly attired and composed lady. And content in that role, or at least adept at giving the appearance of contentment, which Darcy supposed was the same.

The carriage slowed as the road inclined towards the once sleepy fishing village. Salt scent drifted through the windows, and Darcy realized they had almost arrived in Brighton.

Bingley smiled. "Caroline's troubles aside, I am glad we have an excuse to holiday here. It has been two years since I have been to the sea."

"Longer for myself," Darcy said. He had not had occasion for a seaside holiday since well before his father's death. Mr. Darcy the elder had been ill for two years before he succumbed. With Darcy's mother gone six years before, Darcy found himself occupied with caring for his younger sister and the full weight of being master of Pemberley while managing his own grief.

Bingley said, "We shall have a lovely time of it. Bathing. Beautiful women. Let us take our minds away from our heartbreak." Though Bingley affected hearty tone, the sadness lingered in his voice.

Despite Miss Elizabeth having most forcefully rejected his proposal, Darcy could not help hoping for another chance. And how wretched was that? He ought, as Bingley suggested, drown himself in the amusements Brighton offered instead of grasping onto a hope that had been most thoroughly dashed.

Yet Darcy could not control his thoughts.

Miss Bingley and her sister, Mrs. Hurst, had taken lodgings at the New Steyne hotel, overlooking the sea. As the carriage ascended, Darcy looked out over the hillside, down upon the green cornfields leading to the sea. His breath caught. Darcy had always loved the sea. And if Miss Caroline Bingley had fallen, finally, for another man, then perhaps this journey might be a pleasant diversion, as Bingley suggested.

Darcy and Bingley made further idle conversation, and the carriage skirted the Old Steyne promenade.

The carriage circled a fenced enclosure where men and women enjoyed the sunshine and cool sea air. Darcy's gaze passed over the Marlborough Steyne: large, handsome edifices surrounding the enclosure in tan, coral, and flint gray.

With Prinny's passion for architecture, the balance of elegant structures and the beauty of the land surrounded maintained an excellent accord, despite the necessity of constructing most buildings with flint stones and mortar broken only by the brickwork at the doors and windows. The buildings were strong enough to withstand the intense storms and the occasional hurricane blown up from the Caribbean Isles.

Not that there was a cloud in the sky this afternoon. It was clear and blue, reflecting off the sea and fractured kaleidoscope of light. Only a smattering of ladies ambled about in their fashionable walking frocks. The Promenade would fill as evening approached, and the weather cooled.

As they slowed to turn, Darcy's heart caught in his throat as he noted two young ladies walking together. Seeing them from behind, he noted the taller woman's lustrous brown hair. The fall of it, and her way of walking, which he had spent far too long studying when she visited his aunt, reminded him of Miss Elizabeth Bennet.

No! It could not be. What reason did she have to visit Brighton? And the young woman at her side, small and fair-haired with her dress cut scandalously short, just covering her calves, no, Miss Elizabeth would not be seen in such company.

The fair-haired young woman turned, gesturing excitedly towards the carriage, and her companion followed the movement, turning her attention towards him.

It was Miss Elizabeth.

Darcy leaned back on his seat, hoping the curtain would block him from further scrutiny.

Of all the worst misfortune! Why had Miss Elizabeth and the other young woman, whom Darcy could only presume was one of Elizabeth's younger sisters, chosen here to holiday?

"Darcy?" Bingley said, leaning over to look out the window at what had spooked his friend. "What is—? Is that Miss Elizabeth Bennet?"

"I do not know."

"Perhaps Miss Jane Bennet is here as well?" Darcy's stomach clenched at the hope in his friend's voice. Then Bingley sighed and said, "Not that it matters, I suppose."

"I—" To tell his friend about Darcy's potential mistake meant he would have to tell Bingley about the proposal and his disastrous aftermath. Darcy was not willing to risk this without an assurance of Miss Jane Bennet's fidelity.

Or at least continued interest.

"Perhaps Miss Bennet is here for the summer," Darcy mused.

"Do you think she remembers me?"

"We shall see," Darcy said, feeling more and more the arse.

# CHAPTER 3

**M**uch about Brighton recommended itself to Elizabeth. Each day since they had arrived a week ago had offered pleasant weather with only one day of rain. She adored the salty scent of the air and the feel of sand between her toes. The sea, while still chill from winter, cooled her feet as she walked along the shoreline, collecting shells.

Not that she had much occasion to enjoy the seaside. Elizabeth, who would rather have spent her afternoons with her feet dangling into the ocean off of some rock or pier while reading, instead displayed herself along the Old Steyne from morning to mid-afternoon while Lydia amused herself with any who would stand still long enough to endure her chatter.

Mrs. Forster, Lydia and Elizabeth's nominal chaperone, had a head as empty as a conch-shell washed up ashore, and most days she let Lydia wander about with no oversight at all, which left Elizabeth to rein in her sister. A difficult task for Elizabeth even with Jane's help, which Elizabeth could not call upon so far from home.

Elizabeth would have enjoyed Brighton without Lydia's near magical ability to find trouble and place herself square in the center of it. In the past seven days, Lydia had stumbled into in illegal gambling hell while claiming to search for the seaside assembly, which Elizabeth later learned was the following evening. Lydia had swum, full nude, far too close to an outcropping of rock, which, had the day not been so placid, might have caused her grievous wound, and then there was the flirting. She never missed an opportunity to flirt. Lydia flirted with officers, gentlemen and even the boarding house's handsome stable hand who gazed at Elizabeth's younger sister with wide-eyed adoration as he insisted upon helping her ascend and descend from the gig Mr. Forster let for the summer.

With Mrs. Forster, a year and a half Lydia's

senior, smiling magnanimously beside her, Lydia had flirted most shamelessly at Thursday's assembly, and the next morning, on the promenade. They had been forced to return to Mrs. Forster's home for Lydia's parasol, which, though Elizabeth had reminded her to place it by the door so they would not forget it, still languished beneath the bed the two girls shared.

Sharing a bed with Lydia was none near as pleasant as sharing with Jane. Lydia stole the duvet, kicked, snored, and, when caught in a vivid dream, murmured nonsense to the air. The only benefit to sharing a bed was Elizabeth could at least ensure her sister did not steal out in the middle of the night and risk her virtue, such as Mrs. Forster's presence had maintained.

It was on that return trip to the house Lydia spotted Mr. Darcy passing in a carriage.

"Is that Mr. Bingley's carriage?" Lydia exclaimed, pulling on Elizabeth's arm as she waved wildly towards it, ensuring Elizabeth and her sister were impossible to overlook.

*Drat!* Elizabeth thought as she caught sight of Mr. Darcy's profile before he leaned back on his seat.

Worse had been the sudden flutter of happiness

at seeing Mr. Darcy. The gentleman had proposed and, in doing so, insulted every member of her family while also revealing he was responsible for Mr. Bingley's change of heart towards Jane.

Elizabeth did not wish herself happy to see Mr. Darcy. While his letter may have dulled her ire, it should not have shifted her emotions to a genuine approbation. Her heart should not flutter with gladness glimpsing his profile in a passing carriage. It should not hope she crossed his path at a local assembly or while she walked, collecting shells and ignoring Lydia's gossip with Mrs. Forster.

And yet, his profile had spurred both things. Happiness and anticipation.

Lydia said, "That is Mr. Bingley's carriage. Let us find him and ask how he could have hurt Jane so."

"We cannot interrogate Mr. Bingley."

"Why ever not? You told Jane if you saw Mr. Bingley again, you would corner him and find out the exact moment he decided to take his amusement by toying with our sister's heart."

Elizabeth sighed. The worst of it was, Lydia was correct. If Elizabeth had not already learned of Darcy's role in advising his friend against Jane, she would have been eager pull the truth out of Bingley.

But Elizabeth knew why Mr. Bingley had abandoned Jane. And Elizabeth also knew nothing she, as Jane sister, said would hold the same weight as the advice of Mr. Bingley's close friend, whose judgment he trusted over his own.

Lydia asked, "Surely, you're not afraid of Mr. Darcy?"

"No!" Elizabeth was not afraid of Mr. Darcy. He had proposed to her, and she had taken great pleasure in rejecting him.

Elizabeth was not afraid of Mr. Darcy. She was, however, afraid of her response to Mr. Darcy. He had proposed, and she rejected him. He would not propose again. Nor did she want him to. She hardly knew the man, as was plain first in his proposal and later in his letter to her.

Elizabeth said, "I am not convinced speaking with Mr. Bingley, or Mr. Darcy, will be of any use. If Mr. Bingley wished to contact Jane, he could have had his sister write. Perhaps his intent was always to take his amusement in the country and then…"

Elizabeth's throat closed around her lie. Mr. Bingley had not come to Netherfield to amuse himself by breaking ladies' hearts, but Elizabeth could not say that without revealing Darcy's disastrous proposal and her own, albeit justified, misjudgment of him.

Lydia said, "If you have lost your nerve, Lizzy, then I will stand up for Jane."

"I have not lost my nerve," Elizabeth insisted. "I just see no need embarrassing ourselves. Or Jane."

"You are such a stick in the sand. I had thought you more capable of independent thought than Mary."

Elizabeth clenched her hand into a fist. Above, a gull screamed. Elizabeth said, "If Mr. Bingley or Mr. Darcy have anything to say to us, they will seek us out. Jane has already suffered heartbreak enough without us worsening the situation."

Lydia tightened her lips, the left half of her mouth turning downwards. "As you say, Miss Biddle." Her tone was as sharp and sour is a lemon as she called Elizabeth by the name of Meryton's oldest spinster, who was forever offering unwanted advice to the young ladies of the village.

Elizabeth gritted her teeth. She would not let Lydia force her temper. Elizabeth forced herself to take a breath. The carriage had long passed, the dust of it billowing in a gray cloud that obscured its shape. Elizabeth said, "Your parasol."

"Yes, Miss Biddle. It is hot, and a refreshing dip

will set all things to right." Lydia turned her back to Elizabeth and strode towards Mrs. Forster's.

Lydia was plotting something. Elizabeth only hoped in the two days between now and Thursday's assembly, something else would distract her sister. A not unreasonable hope, considering Lydia's short attention span. Perhaps another handsome officer would quirk Lydia a smile, and Lydia would be swept off her feet, clasping her hands at her chest and sighing at the prospect of marriage.

And even if Lydia plotted something for the assembly, Mr. Darcy despised dancing. He would avoid it. He had no more desire to see Elizabeth than she him.

Except Elizabeth wished to see Mr. Darcy.

She shook her head and followed her sister across the promenade.

# CHAPTER 4

W hen Darcy and Bingley arrived at the New Steyne Hotel, Mrs. Hurst and Miss Bingley greeted them in the lobby.

"Charles!" Miss Bingley and Mrs. Hurst sat at a small table. Two cups of tea and a small plate of sliced fruits sat between them.

Caroline rose, smiling as she walked to her brother. "Louisa wrote you to visit us. I'm certain of it." She took her brother's hands and kissed his cheek. "She fears..." Her gaze drifted to Mr. Darcy, and her expression froze a moment before she widened her smile. "Oh! Mr. Darcy. I had not real-ized you were joining my brother for this visit."

Bingley said, "I thought I had written ahead."

Carolyn waved her hand. "The post is sometimes slow to arrive here. It is a more languid lifestyle here in Brighton, especially before Prinny comes to summer."

Darcy nodded. Once the Prince Regent arrived, he expected many things would become more convenient. The Regent had taken a special interest in Brighton, which, in combination with the reputed health benefits of the seaside bathing, had turned this humble fishing village of Brighthelmstone into a large and bustling thoroughfare. Also, its relatively remote location made things less convenient than London proper.

After bowing to both ladies, Darcy said, "I hope I am not an imposition."

"Certainly not," Caroline said.

Mrs. Hurst, who had finished chewing a pastry before rising to greet her brother, said, "We will let the servants know to set another place at dinner tonight."

"Yes." Caroline cocked her head, her expression softening. "Mr. Dunham has agreed to dine with us this evening. I know Louisa wrote you of him and our mutual interest. He wishes to make a good impression upon you, Charles. He would have had us at his house, but they are making renovations, so

I offered for him to dine with us this evening. A friendly dinner. He so wants to make your acquaintance."

Bingley said, "I should like to meet him as well. Louisa mentioned him, but she was scarce in details about this man who has so captured your attention. Bingley glanced at Darcy, "Mr. Darcy went to school with him for a time, he says."

Carolyn's gaze sparkled. "You did! You must tell us everything."

Darcy, not wishing to reveal his misgivings, considering his own brief acquaintanceship with the young man, said, "Mr. Dunham was three years behind me, and we were not close."

"Well, you shall see him again this evening. And I am certain all of us will have much to discuss. Your rooms are on the same floor as ours. I suppose the footmen are taking your luggage up, and then you will wish some time to unpack and perhaps take a walk by the seaside before dinner. We keep to London hours in Brighton and will dine at six."

Darcy nodded. Bingley asked after his sister's health and enjoyment of their time in Brighton, further saying, "A walk should be just the thing. I do love the seaside."

Darcy nodded.

Mrs. Hurst said, "You are fond of the seaside, Mr. Darcy? I had not known you holidayed here."

Darcy said, "Not since I was a young man. Before my father passed."

Mrs. Hurst nodded solemnly.

Mr. Darcy asked, "And your husband, is he here?"

"He has business in town but will join us next week.

Darcy nodded again, and after bowing to the others, said, "I give you leave to enjoy your brother's company."

Caroline smiled and curtsied, her attention quickly returning to her brother as she began to outline her planned activities for the week.

Darcy reveled at Caroline's apparent disinterest in him. Ordinarily, she would be asking his opinion of everything she planned, none too subtly extending an invitation for him to join her through her glances. Now, Darcy was as interesting to Miss Bingley as a chair.

For this alone, Darcy wanted to offer his approbation for the potential match, but that would do neither his friend nor Miss Bingley service.

Darcy went to his rooms, and after speaking with his valet about the evening's dinner, debated a walk along the shoreline. Part of him wondered if his interest in the seaside amble was the hope of meeting Miss Elizabeth and exchanging pleasantries with her.

How could Darcy wish to exchange pleasantries with the woman who had so thoroughly rejected him? He was, in her own words, the last man alive she would consider marrying.

And yet, Darcy hoped.

He hoped his letter to her had altered her perception of him. He hoped he might have the opportunity to prove himself more mutable company and, in that way, gain her regard.

He hoped.

How was it, despite everything, he still had affection for her?

Darcy forced himself to close his eyes and pretend to doze on the hotel bed as his valet, Mr. Walker, unpacked his trunk and arranged his clothing in the closet and chest of drawers. Eventually, Darcy's agitation drove him from the bed. He said curtly, "I will take a walk."

Darcy walked from their hotel and followed the shoreline towards what he estimated was a more populated area of the seaside town.

From his memory, ladies dipped on one side of

the town and gentleman bathed at the opposite. Which was on the east and which on the west; he did not remember. As he walked, in the distance, he noted the bathing machines with their canvas awnings. He slowed and pretended to stare at the sand for shells.

A pair of gentlemen approached from the water, one tall and thin with salt threading through his black hair, the other stocky and brown. He had a blunt nose, square chin and barrel shaped body whose torso seemed too large for his legs.

Darcy nodded to the pair, and they exchanged introductions.

"Good afternoon," the taller man, Mr. Willoughby, shifted to lean on his cane. "Were you hoping to bathe? Kent says the water is pleasant today. I prefer bathing later in the year, when the water is more pleasant, though a cold dip is also healthful." Willoughby pursed his lips.

Darcy waved towards the bathing machines the distance. "Which side is for the gentlemen?"

"That way," Mr. Kent explained, gesturing to his left with his chin.

Mr. Willoughby said, "First time in Brighton, young man?"

"I was here as a boy."

"It is a pleasant place to holiday," Mr. Kent said.

They spoke a bit, remarking on the recent weather. Mr. Willoughby invited Darcy to play cards with him at a local club. "Any evening— though the ladies will regret your absence at Thursday's assembly, should you choose to come that eve." He smiled, a quirky movement that wrinkled the corners of his eyes. "I am not much missed when there is dancing, which I suppose is for the best as my Amelia prefers to keep me to herself."

Darcy said, "I am not married."

"You are young yet. When you wed, I advise you to find a woman who challenges your mind. A handsome face fades with age, but a handsome mind grows finer through the years. And a handsome sense of humor is a jewel beyond compare."

Darcy thought back to Elizabeth's wit and intelligence. Her smile. She had a handsome mind, wit, and a handsome face. He sighed.

Mr. Willoughby's eyes twinkled. "I see."

"No," Darcy protested. "I mean…I have— There is no lady."

The man nodded again, but his lips quirked. "One should not cast away their mallet before they finish the game. Am I right, Matthew?"

Mr. Kent. "You often are, Willoughby."

They nodded again and said their goodbyes. Darcy continued onwards. He passed an old pier and a group of young women who had stopped, one kneeling in the sand as the others exclaimed at her find.

Darcy kneeled and picked up a small, colorful shell. The edges were chipped, and Darcy felt a moment of sympathy for it. A small, battered thing.

Unfortunately, for Darcy, the game with Elizabeth had ended with her clear expression of disapprobation. He stood and turned back to the hotel. His taste for seaside walking had soured.

From behind him, a woman called, "Mr. Darcy!" Darcy looked back. To his mingled joy and dismay, he saw Miss Lydia, another woman, and behind the pair, Miss Elizabeth. Lydia waved.

Darcy could not pretend he had not heard them and break into a shameful dash.

Though they were acquainted, it was improper for Miss Lydia to call out to him so. But Darcy's recall of Miss Lydia and the entire Bennet family was not one of people who composed themselves properly at all occasions. It was something he had found irritating in Hertfordshire. Now, a part of him welcomed Miss Lydia's forwardness.

Darcy turned and said, "Miss Lydia!"

When they were close enough to address at an ordinary volume, he bowed and added, "Miss Elizabeth."

Lydia gave him the briefest curtsy and said, "Mr. Darcy, this is my dear friend, Mrs. Forster. She has allowed us to holiday with her and Col. Forster, an act of both kindness and generosity.

Darcy said, "It is a pleasure to make your acquaintance." He bowed to her again.

Lydia asked, "Are you traveling with Mr. Bingley then?"

"Lydia, we must not harass him about Mr. Bingley."

Darcy said, "Bingley is with me."

"How pleasant," Elizabeth cut in. "Are you enjoying Brighton? I find the sea air most invigorating."

It sat well on her. Her cheeks were flushed, and her hair pleasantly disheveled by the wind.

Darcy said, "I find it very healthful." He had no interest in speaking with Miss Elizabeth of the weather or Mr. Bingley, but better that than an awkward silence. Or worse, for her to cut him directly. Darcy said, "I trust you had a safe journey from Rosings?"

Lydia asked, "You were at Rosings?"

"To visit his aunt," Elizabeth said. "Our paths crossed."

"Oh…" Lydia pressed her lips together. Then she giggled, placing her hand over her mouth as though amused. But the mirth did not touch her eyes. Lydia said, "Elizabeth had not mentioned meeting you at Rosings when she visited Charlotte."

"We hardly spoke," Elizabeth said.

"Yes," Darcy agreed.

Lydia said, "Not even to ask about —?"

"Lydia, we must be on our way. We are meeting Mrs. Forster's friend, remember?"

Mrs. Forster, who had until this point been quiet, her gaze flitting between Lydia, Mr. Darcy, and Miss Elizabeth, said, "It is no trouble. We did not set an exact time."

"And we were walking in the same direction," Miss Lydia noted.

"I am certain Mr. Darcy has business," Miss Elizabeth insisted.

But Miss Lydia ignored her. "Perhaps Mr. Darcy could accompany us?"

Darcy shivered. "It would hardly be appropriate."

"We are acquainted, and Mrs. Forster is capable of serving as chaperone."

Glancing at Mrs. Forster, who was dressed as coquettishly as Miss Lydia and seemed of an age, doubted the woman could chaperone anyone. But it would be impolite to say such.

"Surely, you can accompany us for a little while. Are you and Mr. Bingley staying at the New Steyne Hotel?"

The young woman would have a firm understanding of all the hotels and boarding houses, which made hiding his current residence an impossibility. Darcy nodded. "Bingley and I arrived earlier this afternoon."

Lydia looked back at her sister. "I knew it was Mr. Bingley's carriage!"

"I suppose it must have been," Elizabeth said. She added, "You look well, Mr. Darcy."

Did she intend that as a compliment or merely a comment?

"As do you, Miss Elizabeth."

Miss Lydia let out a long sigh. "You are just alike. I had not seen it before. We know, the sea air is very healthful." Lydia extended her elbow, and Darcy, having no way to avoid offering her the politeness of an escort, captured it.

Mrs. Forster walked at Lydia's right, and Miss Elizabeth, to Darcy's surprise, closed the three steps between where she had been standing to walk at Darcy's left.

Darcy, unsure if he should offer his arm to her as well, stood, staring like a landed fish. Behind them, the wind carried a shout and the faraway call of a gull.

Lydia said, "Mr. Darcy, if you please. I should not like my sister to walk unaccompanied."

Elizabeth opened her mouth, "I am perfectly capable—" But then, she hesitated as Darcy offered his arm. Slowly, she took it. Her scent of lavender mingled with the sea, and Darcy's heart raced. Miss Elizabeth was warm against him. She did not cling like Miss Lydia, but Darcy found Miss Elizabeth's touch enchanting as she looked up at him. "What brings you and Mr. Bingley to Brighton? A holiday?"

"A courtship," Darcy said. Elizabeth stiffened.

Lydia exclaimed, "Mr. Bingley?"

Darcy quickly shook his head. "Miss Bingley."

Elizabeth nodded, "You and Miss Bingley."

"No!" Mr. Darcy interjected again. "Miss Bingley and I are not …suited."

Elizabeth averted her gaze, fixing it on the sand ahead. "Oh," she said.

"Miss Bingley— There is a gentleman she would like her brother to meet."

"She is engaged?"

"Nothing of the sort."

"Our sister Jane has not joined us," Lydia cut in. "Although she may, later, should her health prove up to the travel."

"Miss Bennet is in ill health?"

"No," Elizabeth said. She glared at her sister. "Jane was tired from her travels to London; that is all."

Lydia shook her head. "Jane is not one to share her woes, but she has had a certain melancholic air about her. It came upon her shortly after you and Mr. Bingley departed from Hertfordshire."

"I am certain Mr. Darcy has no interest in our sister's affairs," Miss Elizabeth interjected. "He and Mr. Bingley must have a variety of amusements planned for his holiday."

Lydia asked, "Will you visit with Mr. Wickham?"

Both Darcy and Elizabeth turned to her. Elizabeth asked, "Mr. Wickham?"

"Yes. Mr. Denny told me before we left Meryton; Mr. Wickham is stationed here. I suppose he has been on patrol or some such, because we have not seen him, but—"

Mrs. Forster asked, "Mr. Wickham? I believe he dined with my husband a fortnight back. I thought he was assigned to the records room, but perhaps they sent him to town for further supplies." Mrs. Forster laughed. "I have no understanding of what the brave officers do to protect our shores."

"I will not speak with Mr. Wickham," Darcy said.

"Nor I," Elizabeth added. "I have it on authority he is not worth our time."

Lydia's eyes narrowed. "It would be improper, I suppose."

Elizabeth stiffened again. "I do not wish to speak of Mr. Wickham."

"I am sorry, sister. I had thought you fond of him, before."

"You are mistaken."

At least Darcy knew Miss Elizabeth had read his letter and taken his words to heart. His cheeks warmed.

"Mr. Darcy," Mrs. Forster said with an overly bright smile, "If you are just arrived, there is an assembly every Thursday, should you wish to become acquainted with some of the others on holiday here."

Elizabeth said, "I am certain Mr. Darcy has no interest in an assembly."

"What a shame. Lydia, Elizabeth, and I attended last week and we intend to dance again Thursday."

Mr. Bingley is fond of dancing, and I may join him."

Miss Elizabeth said, with the barest hint of her usual vigor, "To stand and glower, I suppose?"

"Or perhaps to dance. And glower." Darcy's lips twitched.

Miss Elizabeth smiled, and then seeming surprised at her own amusement, put her hand over her mouth and schooled her features. "Was that a jest, Mr. Darcy?"

"Only at my own expense."

"I had thought..." Miss Elizabeth shook her head. "I should think many young ladies would be pleased to have both you and Mr. Bingley attend. Often, at these affairs, the ladies outnumber the gentlemen, and for those of us who enjoy dancing, a partner is essential."

"I enjoy dancing with an agreeable partner." Darcy ventured.

Miss Elizabeth, for all of her hostility at his proposal, was now affecting quite an amenable manner. Almost as if she wished to speak with him.

Perhaps Darcy's letter had softened her heart. Not that she would accept a second proposal, or even a dance from him, but...

Hope was a foolish and painful thing.

Darcy said, "I will make certain Mr. Bingley knows of the assembly. It will give him great joy to dance."

It would give Bingley great joy, and Darcy himself, if Miss Elizabeth attended.

They walked a while longer, exchanging idle conversation. Mrs. Forster asked him about his visit, and Miss Lydia attempted to turn the subject back to her sisters, both of them. By the time Darcy returned to his hotel, he was aching with anxiety and unsaid words.

He dared not flirt with Miss Elizabeth again, considering the watchful eye of her younger sister and equally youthful chaperone. And while the conversation was effusive, it set Darcy's teeth on edge. But Darcy did all in his power to show kindness and interest in the young ladies' conversation. Given this second chance, he would show himself a gentleman for Elizabeth. And if his reward was the slight quirking of Elizabeth lips, the furrow in her brow and then softening of her eyes, then perhaps his efforts were worth suffering useless conversation with simpering idiots.

Elizabeth excepted.

Hope was indeed a foolish and painful thing.

# CHAPTER 5

When it was clear Mr. Darcy had walked out of earshot, Mrs. Forster turned to Elizabeth, hands shaking as she grabbed Elizabeth's and pulled her close. "What a remarkable man!"

Lydia said, "Maybe there is something to the sea air. Mr. Darcy is much warmer here than he was at Netherfield. And Lizzy..." Lydia cocked her head. "What happened at Rosings, Lizzy? You and he are different with each other than before."

"It is your imagination," Elizabeth said. "Nothing happened at Rosings."

Mrs. Forster asked, "Has Mr. Darcy fallen in love?"

"No!" Elizabeth said.

Lydia let out a peal of laughter. "He considers Lizzy tolerable."

"Mr. Darcy did not treat Elizabeth as a woman he considered tolerable."

"He is a gentleman," Elizabeth said. "It was politeness."

"Perhaps he has decided you are admirably tolerable, Lizzy. As opposed to merely tolerable."

Elizabeth pinched the bridge of her nose. Mrs. Forster was far too perceptive. If she convinced Lydia there was something more between Elizabeth and Mr. Darcy, Lydia would not rest until she had found out everything that was a scandal or secret. Once Lydia had scented something juicy, she did not rest. And if she told their mother Elizabeth had rejected Mr. Darcy's proposal, Elizabeth would not have a moment's peace.

So Elizabeth forced a smile and lied. "Yes, admirably tolerable. At best."

Mrs. Forster said, "Well. If Mr. Darcy is unwed, and so gallant, and there is no agreement between you, then another lady will better suit."

"No lady could suit Mr. Darcy." Elizabeth said. "He has only met four he considers accomplished. I suspect one is his sister and the other his odious aunt."

"The Lady Catherine de Bourgh!" Lydia exclaimed in a fair imitation of Mr. Collin's obsequious tones. "A more remarkable paragon of wisdom, kindness, and noble carriage could not exist in this world."

Mrs. Forster laughed.

Elizabeth feigned merriment even as her thoughts strayed to Mrs. Forster's words. 'Another lady will better suit.'

The idea of Mr. Darcy courting another woman made Elizabeth's skin itch. She scratched her arm. She said, "I do not wish to speak further of Mr. Darcy. I am more interested in tonight's dinner. The Brigadier is hosting us and his officers at his home tonight, is he not?"

Mrs. Forster said, "Yes! Though one never knows until they call the hour which officers will attend. They are all so absorbed in their work. It is such a joy to enjoy a proper meal with them." Mrs. Forster went on at length about the menu, and Lydia, distracted by the prospect of handsome men, all available for flirtation, made no further mention of Mr. Darcy.

Thank heaven!

Elizabeth asked who was attending, and most importantly, if the frocks they had brought would impress the gentlemen, considering they had worn their best gowns the previous week.

Lydia clapped her hands together. "I saw some ribbon at Sunday's market in one of the shops, and I believe it will well accentuate my waist."

Miss Forster said, "We must go immediately. We will need time to dress, have our hair arranged, and have a servant make the alterations."

Shopping and preparing herself for the banquet was an adequate distraction from meeting Mr. Darcy on the beach.

Lydia made no further comment about Mr. Darcy, and Elizabeth was glad to put the entire thing behind her when they arrived at Brigadier Holmes' home.

Mrs. Holmes was a thin, pale woman with a rounded belly. Her eyes lit up as she saw Mrs. Forster. "Amelia!" she said, taking the other woman's hands.

They whispered to each other and Mrs. Forster said, "Go ahead. I will be along."

Mr. Forster, Elizabeth and Lydia continued into

the house. More officers arrived after them and, to Elizabeth's dismay, one was Wickham.

Lydia leaned to Elizabeth and whispered, "Is that Mr. Wickham? He looks very smart in his reds, does he not?"

Elizabeth made no comment.

Lydia added. "And handsome."

The ladies and gentlemen arranged themselves in order of rank, which put Col. Forster, his wife, and six couples further ahead than the Bennet sisters. Worse, Mr. Wickham was across from Elizabeth.

Mr. Wickham smiled and said to them both, "Miss Elizabeth, Miss Lydia, this is an unexpected pleasure."

Lydia smiled, looking up at him through her lashes. She took a deep breath, and her bosom heaved. "Mr. Denny mentioned you were stationed here. My sister and I are glad we have the pleasure of your company, are we not, Lizzy?"

Elizabeth wanted to jam her elbow into her sister's side, but such a gesture would invite questions.

Elizabeth said, "It is a surprise." She nodded to the officer across from Lydia. He was a young man, coltish, with light brown hair and too large hands and feet. He bowed and smiled wide with large teeth.

"Miss Lydia?" he said. "It is my great pleasure to meet you."

Lydia gave him a brief curtsy. "Likewise, sir."

"Albert. Albert Stewart. Mr. Stewart."

"Mr. Stewart," Lydia said.

"Col. Forster said you and your sister are guests of Mrs. Forster. How are you enjoying Brighton?"

"Healthful," Lydia said.

"Yes. That is as Brigadier Holmes says when he leads our morning drills."

"I trust it is not too strenuous," Lydia said, but her gaze focused on Mr. Wickham. "They do not force you to rise too early?"

Mr. Wickham said, "No hour is too early in the defense of our shores."

The twit. How had Elizabeth found him sympathetic?

Mr. Wickham said, "Am I correct to address you as Miss Elizabeth? Is Miss Jane Bennet here? I have not seen her."

"Jane is at Longbourn," Elizabeth said shortly.

"A shame," Mr. Wickham said. "I much like

how the syllables Miss E-liz-a-beth roll from the tongue. You have a lovely given name."

Elizabeth forced a laugh. "I have always felt my name most ordinary."

"Mr. Wickham," Lydia said. "Mr. Denny said they sent you here, but after a week, I had worried you had been transferred."

"I was ordered to London to deliver some important papers to—" Mr. Wickham shook his head. "I cannot say. But it was critical. You understand, Miss Lydia."

Lydia smiled, fluttering her lashes. "How brave! When I was a child, we were much afeared of the French invasion. Now, we do not speak of such things, but I suppose it is because men like you work so hard to keep us safe. It is admirable. So admirable."

Elizabeth wished she had taken Lydia aside before the dinner and given her fair warning about Mr. Wickham. Elizabeth did not like the way the older man was admiring her sister. Lydia was only turned sixteen. And she had the sense of one two years younger with the body of a woman two years older. Knowing that Mr. Wickham had seduced Mr. Darcy's sister did not make Elizabeth comfortable in the slightest about how Mr. Wickham now toyed with Lydia's attention.

Mr. Wickham turned his attention to Elizabeth. "And you, Miss Elizabeth Bennet, do you also think our work admirable?"

"A soldier's work, yes, defending our shores, is very admirable."

Mr. Wickham held out his arm, and Elizabeth could not ignore him without disrupting the atmosphere of the dinner, which meant she had to endure Mr. Wickham's touch. He smiled at her, eyes glittering.

How had she ever imagined him attractive or pitiable? Now that she knew of his past, she noted the calculation in his gaze as he smiled at her, and then looked over the other ladies in his view. He asked, "Is that a new frock?"

"I cannot say," Elizabeth said, looking at the lady, a blonde with bright red cheeks, who had distracted Mr. Wickham's attention.

Mr. Wickham turned his attention back to her with a laugh. "I must apologize, my gaze wanders sometimes, but my mind was enamored of how the blue of that fabric complements your eyes."

Elizabeth glanced down at her gown. She had also liked how the deep blue pattern complimented her eyes. Now, she wished she had worn a less flattering garment. One faded brown and frayed at the sleeves and hems.

Elizabeth forced a smile and said, "We acquired a few things in town."

"It suits you."

Elizabeth nodded. She was not inclined to thank him for the compliment. She was not inclined toward speaking with him at all. But she could not cut him without calling attention to her reasons. Elizabeth said, "Your work must be a very interesting."

Mr. Wickham shrugged. "Not as interesting as the company here. I heard rumors of how raucous affairs were in Brighton, but I have found my work here most salubrious. The company is refined and the sea air reputed to be healthful."

Lydia, interjected from behind Elizabeth, "Very healthful. Mr. Darcy and Lizzy were both effusive on the quality of the air here."

Wickham's gloved fingers, which rested on Elizabeth's forearm, tensed. "Mr. Darcy is here?" His expression was bland, but Elizabeth heard the edge in his mild tone. Or perhaps she imagined it, knowing their history. She affected a wide-eyed gaze and said, with a giggle most unlike her, "Yes. Our hostess, Mrs. Forster, Lydia and I happened upon Mr. Darcy this afternoon while collecting shells. He is here with Mr. Bingley."

"Mr. Darcy said for a courtship," Lydia said.

"Mr. Darcy? Courting?"

"He is not courting," Elizabeth declared. "He is accompanying Mr. Bingley, who I'm certain you also remember from your time at Meryton." Elizabeth hated to give Mr. Wickham any information about Mr. Darcy, but if she did not interject, then Lydia would continue burbling like a brook, sharing not only Mr. Darcy's words but also her own suppositions. Elizabeth said, "I suspect as a chance for Mr. Darcy to take a step away from his burdens."

They entered the dining room. Mr. Wickham laughed. "Yes, we all must defer to Mr. Darcy's *burdens*, must we not?"

Thankfully, they parted from each other to sit opposite at the long dining table. Mr. Wickham would be seated opposite Elizabeth. Looking over the table, her hopes of a large flower display or elaborate candelabra between them were dashed.

Mrs. Forster and Brigadier Holmes' wife were friends, and Mrs. Forster had made a point of suggesting an open atmosphere. Mrs. Forster wished the ladies and gentlemen at the tables to socialize.

In the week since Elizabeth and Lydia had arrived, Mrs. Forster had shown herself the avid match-maker. Much to Lydia's delight and Elizabeth's annoyance.

Elizabeth had not wished to join her sister in Brighton, but she recognized her value in preserving Lydia's reputation. Mrs. Forster's inclination to thrust the two girls in front of every gentleman whose path they crossed, in combination with Lydia's incessant flirting, made the danger to Lydia's virtue more pronounced, Elizabeth suspected. And whenever Elizabeth asked Lydia to be more circumspect, she waved her older sister off. "It is all in good fun," she would say, lifting her fan and fluttering at her neck and bosom.

If Lydia's frivolity did not reflect ill on Elizabeth, Jane, and all of her sisters, Elizabeth might have let Lydia fall. But Lydia's actions reflected on all the Bennet girls, so Elizabeth devoted herself to stopping Lydia from making an irrevocable mistake.

Which meant Elizabeth could not continue keeping the substance of Mr. Darcy's confession from Lydia. Nor could Elizabeth state the warning came from Mr. Darcy. Lydia, even when she intended to keep a secret, often blabbed.

Elizabeth took a slow breath and sat, allowing

the footmen to push in her chair. Lydia was young and had an exuberant nature. Elizabeth could only hope the girl would age out of the worst of her frivolity. Though Elizabeth and Jane had both been out at sixteen, Lydia would have benefited from another year or two of finishing. Or at least an interest in life beyond gossip and fashion plates.

They engaged in pleasantries, Mr. Stewart complemented Lydia's ribbon, which caused her to giggle and flutter her fan. Elizabeth was grateful the young man's flattery distracted Lydia from Mr. Wickham. Elizabeth regretted not warning her sister upon hearing Mr. Wickham was stationed in Brighton. She could have taken Lydia aside before the meal and said something. She could not betray Mr. Darcy's confidence, but somehow she had to convince her sister—

After dinner, she would.

The soup was served, and when Elizabeth had finished half of her bowl, Mr. Wickham asked, "Did Mr. Darcy mention how long he intended to visit Brighton?"

"No."

"I suppose he had to speak with you, considering your paths crossed."

Elizabeth sipped her soup. "I suppose."

"I must apologize. Speaking of Darcy has put you off of your food."

Elizabeth said, "The soup is excellent."

Mr. Wickham's eyes narrowed. "So it is. Enough of dismal topics. How are you and Miss Lydia enjoying Brighton?"

"Oh Mr. Wickham," Lydia effused, "We are having a lovely time! I do so adore bathing. And collecting shells. I have already made a frame for our mother and for Kitty. I suppose Elizabeth is working on something for Jane. She and Jane were always the closest because of their age, though, I suppose, it's not in Jane's nature to favor any one above another."

"Not even Mr. Bingley? Miss Bennet and Mr. Bingley had come to some accord."

Elizabeth said, "We are not in the habit of gossiping about our sisters." She glared at Lydia.

Mr. Stewart cut in, "How many sisters have you?"

Elizabeth, grateful to change the subject, said, "Together, we number five."

The man's eyebrows raised. "Five? What a merry household you must have!"

Elizabeth said, "Yes, but, with five of us girls to

find husbands, and our estate entailed to our cousin, it is rather a trial for our mother."

Lydia took a sharp breath through her teeth. "Lizzy!"

Elizabeth recognized she was causing both Lydia and herself trouble by explaining their family's precarious financial state, but better that than to have Mr. Wickham think he could gain a fortune in ruining Lydia.

"I would never wish to present myself under false pretenses," Elizabeth said, recognizing she sounded more like Mary than herself. Mary would not risk being ruined by Mr. Wickham.

Lydia said, "Our father has set us up well enough. I do not think it is so desperate as my sister states."

Elizabeth smiled, "Lydia, would it not be better for us to be loved as ourselves and not for some allotment of funds and we bring?"

"Yes, of course," Lydia muttered. She took another sip of her soup, her spoon scraping over the few remaining drops at the bottom.

Mr. Stewart said, "I think it better to marry for true affection and a commonality of spirit, but a lady wishes her husband to keep her in the same comforts as her father's household."

Elizabeth said, "We are not so mercenary is that." Though, many women were. Mrs. Bennet certainly.

Mr. Stewart smiled, his expression softening as he stared at Elizabeth with what Elizabeth prayed was not a burgeoning affection. "Not all women, I suppose. Just as not all men are enamored of a woman's dowry to the exclusion of her other qualities."

"Absolutely not," Mr. Wickham said the last. ""I cannot claim temptation to marry from a woman's dowry alone."

Elizabeth gripped her spoon. "You cannot?"

"Has someone painted me as a devil in your mind? I can only think of one who might, and noting us side-by-side, one could make her own determination about the amiability of our respective natures."

Elizabeth said, "Yes. One could." She turned her attention to the young officer. "Mr. Stewart, are you also assigned to records?"

Elizabeth rather liked Mr. Stewart, even if Lydia was indifferent. If Lydia was to flirt, better to focus her attention on this man, who, while not as handsome of features as Mr. Wickham, seemed a more acceptable sort. And young, considering his large hands and feet, not yet grown into his frame.

The man nodded shyly. "I would have preferred a more active posting, but my two brothers are serving with Nelson, and my mother refused to send a third son off at eight to serve as a ship's boy, so I was tutored, and I write with a clean hand."

Elizabeth smiled. "You still must train to keep in good fighting form. Should Napoleon invade, we will need all hands."

Mr. Stewart's expression brightened at Elizabeth's words. "Yes. We are England's last line of defense before her people.

The rest of the meal went as smoothly as Elizabeth could hope, though Elizabeth noted Mr. Wickham's attention on her through the rest of the meal.

Mr. Wickham was subtle about it, taking care to make conversation with all around him while Lydia simpered; and Mr. Stewart attempted to engage Elizabeth in conversation, at first about clothing, and then, at Lydia's loud direction, books. Mr. Stewart held no fault for Elizabeth's animosity towards Mr. Wickham and her frustration with her sister. Elizabeth, not wishing to slight the young man, indulged him and they conversed, if one could call his asking questions and her discussing them at length, a conversation.

As they served the dessert course, Elizabeth's cheeks ached from forced smiles, and her stomach churned beneath Mr. Wickham's scrutiny. She wished she was not a lady but a gentleman who could, after the meal was complete, challenge her opponent to fisticuffs and settle the situation directly. But she was a lady, and she would not endanger the reputation of Mr. Darcy's sister. Miss Darcy did not deserve to have her greatest shame brought to public life. Nor did Mr. Darcy, who had done all in his power to protect the young girl. Though Elizabeth had never met her, she also felt protective of the shy young lady whom Mr. Darcy loved.

The ladies and gentlemen retired to separate rooms to converse.

Mrs. Forster rushed over to Elizabeth and Lydia as soon as she was able. "Mrs. Holmes was not aware of the change to the guest list until after the gentleman had arrived. If she had told me—I would have had you seated elsewhere—"

Lydia laughed. "It was nothing. We had a most engaging meal. Was it not, Lizzy?"

Elizabeth needed to take Lydia aside and share

her reservations, but she could not do that in front of the other ladies. Already, two of Mrs. Forster's friends had shushed their own conversations, and they listened, pretending interest in their drinks.

Elizabeth said, "All was well." She would have to speak with Lydia later. Preferably before the men finished their cigars and joined the ladies again.

Mr. Wickham had been far too interested in Mr. Darcy's whereabouts. Elizabeth wondered if she ought to find some way of warning Mr. Darcy, perhaps if she walked the shore near his hotel, they might cross paths again? Thanks to Lydia, Mr. Darcy knew of Mr. Wickham's presence. And Miss Georgiana had not accompanied Mr. Darcy to Brighton, so he had nothing to fear. If anything, it was Lydia who was in the most danger.

Elizabeth added, "Mr. Stewart was excellent company."

Lydia shrugged. "He was dull but pleasant." She and Mrs. Forster began an animated conversation about the evening's guests and planned parlor games. "Mrs. Holmes is feeling ill. I suggested she take a rest, and I thought perhaps a charade, but with so many it would become cumbersome. Besides, it is important to allow ladies and gentlemen to mingle with each other, and one cannot do that while silently creating a historical scene. Perhaps cards then? We played cards last week, and I should hate for the guests to think me uninspired."

"Everyone enjoyed cards last week," Elizabeth said. "Entertainment need not be inspired."

"Ignore Lizzy," Lydia said. "She is sour because Mr. Wickham is not so odious as she pretended. Or perhaps she is jealous."

"I am not jealous," Elizabeth said.

Lydia laughed. "A woman always says such things when she is jealous. What benefit would she have admitting it?"

"What benefit would she have admitting it when she was not?"

Mrs. Forster asked, "What has Mr. Wickham done to earn your disapprobation, Miss Elizabeth?"

Lydia said, "All the handsome men earn Lizzy disapprobation. Ask Mr. Darcy."

Elizabeth wanted to strangle her sister. She said, "Lydia, if you have a moment, I should like to speak with you alone."

"I can leave you to yourselves," Mrs. Forster said, taking a step back.

Lydia said, "No. Whatever you wish to speak of

with me, Lizzy, we can do so in front of Mrs. Forster."

Elizabeth wished she could strangle her sister. Jaw aching as she smiled again, Elizabeth demurred, "Later then."

Lydia could only get into so much trouble with Mr. Wickham while playing a game of cards in front of a dozen observers.

Elizabeth hoped.

# CHAPTER 6

**D**arcy returned to the hotel with an hour to spare. He wished he could avoid the meal. He disliked dining with strangers, and he was preoccupied with the conversation he had with Miss Elizabeth earlier on the beach. Considering how had she rejected this proposal, he had feared she might cut him directly, but his letter must have softened her heart. She was not only polite but warm. And Darcy had made special pains to show interest in Elizabeth's sister and their friend. Frankly, more interest than Miss Elizabeth had shown in her companions.

Darcy was no expert in reading Miss Elizabeth's moods, though he had gained some knowledge and studying her in Hertfordshire and following her, even walking with her, at Rosings. Her opinion of Mr. Wickham had changed. Darcy was grateful for that, and happy she had felt comfortable enough to take his arm and rest her fingers atop his as they walked.

Given the chance, Darcy would have walked with Miss Elizabeth the length of the shore, saying as little or as much as she chose.

Hope was a foolish thing.

Darcy bathed and dressed into the clothes his valet had set out. Mr. Walker tied Darcy's cravat in an intricate knot, straightening it and brushing his clothes. Though Darcy would not normally wear Hessians for a meal with Bingley's family, he would not present himself as less than his best.

Mr. Walker said, "Miss Bingley's current suitor may be the son of a baron, but you are the nephew of an earl, and it would do well for him to recognize this."

Darcy smiled and said, "I thank you for your work." While Darcy was more concerned with the man, it would be good for Mr. Dunham to recognize Miss Caroline Bingley had friends amongst the older families. Darcy might not be a Lord, but if he needed to have a discussion with the man, best to do so from strength."

When Mr. Darcy left his room, Mrs. Hurst was pacing in front of his door.

"Mr. Darcy?" Mrs. Hurst asked. She was pale, and sweat sheened across her forehead as she pinched her forefinger between the index finger and thumb of her opposite hand.

Worried, Mr. Darcy took a step towards her. "Are you well?"

Mrs. Hurst was dressed for dinner in a gown of pale blue and white. Her hair, light brown and thin, had been painstakingly curled, though the curls drooped.

Mrs. Hurst said, "I should not gossip. My sister says you are very circumspect and do not share confidences."

What could trouble Mrs. Hurst enough to confess to Mr. Darcy and not her own sister?

Mr. Darcy said, "I will keep any confidence you give me."

"My sister's gone ahead, and I fear, if what I heard is true, it will break her heart."

Mr. Darcy asked, "What have you heard?"

He wished he could invite her into his room for

more private conversation, but though she was married, it would not reflect well for her to be seen entering and exiting an unmarried man's room. Especially not with her husband still away in London.

Mrs. Hurst fiddled with the filigreed rope holding her small purse hanging from her elbow and said, "The Baron has made some poor investments. Stocks, I believe. It is not trade, but—" Mrs. Hurst shook her head. "I do not know exactly, but I have heard from Mrs. Diamond who spoke with Mrs. Richardson who is close with Baron Dunham's sister... The Baron lost quite a lot of money, and should he fail to pay his creditors, his estate will be entailed away from him."

"Are you certain?" Mr. Darcy's solicitor had found nothing of this, though the Dunhams' estate and lands were south of London, in Berkshire and aside from attending school together, Darcy had no other connections to the place.

Mrs. Hurst said, "I can be sure of nothing. I heard it from Mrs. Diamond. Perhaps she mistook the name, or was otherwise mistaken. But if it is true, my sister puts her future in grave danger by pursuing this match."

"Have you told her of what you've learned?"

"Caroline will hear no more from me on the

subject of Mr. Dunham. She knows I do not approve. I feel he is too ostentatious and too forward. And I sense there something hidden in his manners. He pretends spontaneity, but there's always a calculation to him. And he is too charming. He tells my sister what she wishes to hear. I believe he has been writing her in secret. He has made no proposal, but he takes such improper action. Caroline believes it a sign of his infatuation, but I believe he is more interested in a connection to our wealth than the assets my sister possesses. There is something nefarious in too charming a man, you understand."

Darcy did not, but no woman would accuse him of being too charming. The last woman he attempted to woo had rejected him flatly. Darcy said, "If Mr. Dunham is in financial distress, there will be signs of it. Signs your sister would note."

"Ordinarily, yes. But she has always wanted a title. Even a woman as sensible as my sister can be distracted by promises of a title."

Darcy could not doubt that. He said, "I shall write to my solicitor and ask him to look into this matter. And we shall keep a watchful eye on Mr. Dunham, just in case."

Mrs. Hurst took a long breath. Pulling a handkerchief from her purse, she dabbed her eyes before looking up at Darcy with a tremulous smile. "Thank you. You are a true friend to us, Mr. Darcy. I had always hoped you and my sister might find some accord, but..." She shook her head. "Whether a brother in truth or a brother in heart, you are one to us."

Darcy smiled. He held out his arm, and Mrs. Hurst took it. Darcy was both gratified by Mrs. Hurst's trust and burdened by it. But he owed Bingley. He would write his solicitor of this, and, with luck, find this gossip to be only a rumor. But Mr. Darcy understood, from observing his mother, Lady Matlock, and Aunt Catherine, how well the ladies of the household knew what their husbands thought of their own business, and how effortlessly news spread when one lady discovered something of interest.

Or scandalous.

When Darcy and Mrs. Hurst arrived at the private room Bingley had to let for dining, Bingley and Miss Caroline Bingley had already arrived. Miss Bingley wore what Darcy recognized as the latest London fashion, black ostrich feather fan in hand.

"Louisa! I had looked for you," Miss Bingley

said. "I should have realized Mr. Darcy was being chivalrous." Darcy bowed to her, and Miss Bingley smiled. "Mr. Darcy, it is a pleasure to see you again, and after such a short time. Charles had mentioned you and Mr. Dunham attended school together, and though you say you do not remember him well, I am certain he shall be glad to happen upon a fellow schoolmate."

Mr. Darcy said, "It shall delight me to reacquaint myself."

Miss Caroline said, "There is nothing you can tell me? No anecdote of any kind?"

"He likes sweets."

Miss Caroline smiled. "I believe he still does. Louisa remembers when he happened upon us having tea in the main dining room at the hotel; he helped himself liberally to the fruit tarts. He mentioned having dined at one of the Regent's soirées, where they served a special pastry coated in hard caramel. Mr. Dunham's eyes lit when he spoke of the taste."

"He never told us what brought him to the New Steyne that afternoon," Mrs. Hurst said.

Miss Bingley laughed. "Oh, Louisa! What does it matter? He was most pleasant company, even you agreed. Mr. Darcy, are you fond of sweets?"

"Not especially," Darcy said.

"He eats licorice," Bingley interjected with a laugh. "It is his only vice."

Miss Caroline said, "Mr. Dunham is fortunate. Whatever sweets he indulges himself with do not cling to his frame." Miss Bingley sighed. "If only I were so lucky. I must pay careful attention to my food else risk my figure."

Miss Bingley spoke matter-of-factly, and not in the flirtatious tone Darcy was used to from her. Further, Miss Bingley did not stare up at Mr. Darcy, her gaze insisting he compliment her figure or clothing or any other thing about her. Darcy found it refreshing.

If Darcy were lucky, Mr. Dunham would be exactly as he appeared, a besotted suitor with whom Miss Bingley could build a pleasant life far from Mr. Darcy.

But Darcy doubted Miss Bingley could find a true affection with someone without adequate funds to support her. Miss Bingley, for all of her faults, was not one to misjudge a person's wealth. It explained why she had attached herself so firmly and quickly to Darcy himself.

Mr. Dunham arrived precisely ten minutes before the meal was scheduled to be served. A footman announced him, and he entered, carrying a bouquet of purple and white violets. He bowed. "Miss Bingley," he said, handing her the flowers.

Miss Bingley's cheeks flushed as she held them to her nose and breathed.

Darcy felt it forward to give her the flowers in the evening before a meal instead of sending them the next morning with his note of thanks. But he could not deny Miss Bingley's obvious delight at both the flowers, and, Darcy suspected, his senti-ment: white for innocence, violet for thoughts of love.

"And this must be your brother," Mr. Dunham added, inclining his head towards Bingley who offered his usual wide and affable smile.

"Mr. Dunham."

Miss Bingley said, "We shall set these on the table. They will add a lovely engagement of the eyes and scent."

"My thanks," Mr. Dunham said. "I know it more proper to have them sent in the morning, but I admit selfishness in wishing to see your face as you received them."

"It is a selfishness I can well tolerate," Miss Bingley said, taking another breath of the bouquet.

Mr. Dunham did not dress like a man facing

destitution. He wore the latest London fashion: his shirt was the finest cambric, ruffled for the evening with a starched collar and an intricately tied cravat. His waistcoat was black for evening, double-breasted. Hessians gleamed over his pantaloons which were also immaculate and tailored so finely they hid well the slight rounding in his gut.

Though if the financial troubles were recent, they might not yet reflect in Mr. Dunham's wardrobe.

Miss Bingley said, "My sister, Mrs. Hurst, you know, and this is my brother's dear friend, Mr. Fitzwilliam Darcy. I believe you and he attended school together for a time?"

Mr. Dunham's gaze rested on Darcy, and he hesitated. "Yes," he said, "I thought there was something familiar to your face. Darcy was a number of years ahead of me. I do not believe we shared three, perhaps four conversations?"

"If that."

"Darcy was not much for idle conversation. Still, we would rather have had him as our head boy than Chelten. Rumor was you were firm but fair, only meting out punishments with cause."

Darcy's cheeks warmed. He had assumed the

younger boys resented him as he resented the elders who had disciplined him.

"Punishments?" Miss Bingley cocked her head.

"In school, the older boys manage the younger," Darcy said. "But a young man's education is not the proper subject of dinner conversation.

Darcy again wished Mrs. Hurst's gossip was in error. He liked this cheerful, well-dressed man. If Mr. Dunham adored Miss Bingley enough to do away with proprieties, Darcy wanted to wish them both happy.

They sat in order of rank, with Darcy across from Miss Bingley, Mr. Dunham across from Mrs. Hurst, and Mr. Bingley at the table's head. Neither Mr. Dunham nor Miss Bingley seemed pleased with the seating arrangement though they were close enough to easily speak with the other. Mr. Dunham adroitly conversed with the two ladies, Miss Bingley with more enthusiasm than her sister, Darcy observed.

They had their soup, summer squash, and then began the first course.

While Darcy would have preferred to let his solicitor make all inquiries into Mr. Dunham, it might take a fortnight or more to receive information from town, which meant he could not ignore the opportunity to question the man, as subtly as he was able, about his family's situation.

As he mulled over the best way to manage this, Mrs. Hurst asked, "Mr. Dunham, how much longer do you expect your renovations to continue? I had thought they would be finished by now?"

"So had I!" Mr. Dunham shook his head. "The men had to send to town for some things, and the new wall silk was delayed. I do not know what my dear mother was thinking, having the place all done at once. I am confined to my office with bedding on the sofa which is a near half a foot too short. I wake either to neck-ache or tingling in my feet, or both."

If the Dunham family had fallen upon hard times, an excellent way to keep visitors away was to claim their home was being remodeled. At the same time, nothing about Mr. Dunham's story was implausible.

Mrs. Hurst said, "Perhaps you should let a small house or a room. I believe you can find a room here. The New Steyne accommodated Charles and Mr. Darcy."

"I was not sent on holiday, but to ensure the restorations went as planned." Mr. Dunham cut into his fish. "I would rather have my eyes on them.

And if the weather is fair, I sleep on the boat. The rocking of the sea is very pleasant."

Mr. Bingley leaned forward, placing his fork back on his plate as he asked, "What sort of boat? I am fond of yachting, though I hardly have the opportunity."

"Then you must join me. It is a large vessel, wonderful for a pleasure cruise. Some friends will join me Friday, if you and your sisters, and Mr. Darcy of course, would like to join. It will be an afternoon jaunt with dinner on the sea."

"How delightful!" Miss Bingley said, clapping her hands together. "Yes, we must go."

Bingley smiled indulgently at his sister. "I suppose I cannot refuse."

"Oh Charles!" Miss Bingley grinned. "This will be a lovely excursion."

"Lovelier for the company," Mr. Dunham said.

Miss Bingley's cheeks pinked again. Darcy turned his gaze to his fish.

As the meal continued, Mr. Dunham continued flattering Miss Bingley. His remarks were just shy of improper, and Miss Bingley enjoyed the attention. She smiled and laughed, tossing her head so that her curls fell in a flattering manner about her face.

Darcy was grateful the woman's attention was not directed at him this time.

Darcy managed only one further inquiry about Mr. Dunham's father.

"Yes, he and mother are well," Mr. Dunham said. "They have much work on our estate what with managing the new farming equipment. The tenants are slow to change, he says." Dunham laughed, but there was a tightness about his lips.

Darcy said, "I have found it the same, sometimes."

"Your father.... I must convey my condolences. He has recently passed, has he not?"

"It is near two years," Darcy said. He turned his gaze to the dessert, an assortment of sliced fruits and biscuits. He and his father had not been close with Darcy being sent away for school at twelve and his father burying himself in his work to keep from thinking of his wife, whom Darcy reminded him too much of, both in appearance and temperament.

But his father's absence was like a missing tooth. A space he constantly touched, waiting for something to fill the gap. Except, unlike a milk tooth, nothing new would fill the place. Often Darcy felt like an imposter on his own lands, and he had feared pushing the tenants too far in taking up new equipment. They knew their business better than he did, no matter how many books Darcy might read to improve his knowledge of agriculture and animal husbandry. "I miss him," Darcy said. "Pemberley misses him," he added, recognizing greater truth in the latter statement.

The meal ended. Bingley lamented the lack of a parlor or smoking room, "Except that which is open to the public."

With clear regret, Mr. Dunham claimed an early morning. Miss Bingley caught her brother's eye, and they rose and accompanied Mr. Dunham to the door. He left with promises to send ahead more information about the location and time for their pleasure jaunt.

Miss Bingley said, "I hope we will see you all at tomorrow's assembly."

"It will give me the greatest pleasure to attend, and if obliged, claim a place on your dance card. There is a new dance from town the Regent favors, and—"

"I have heard it called scandalous!" Mrs. Hurst cut in.

"Perhaps it would be best to observe first," Mr. Dunham said, his eyes twinkling. "Darcy, Bingley, tomorrow then?"

"We must do our part," Bingley said with a grin. "We would not wish the ladies shorted of gentlemen for dancing. Right Darcy?"

"Right," Darcy said, smothering a sigh. Now he would have no choice but to attend. If thoughts of seeing Miss Elizabeth again made the duty less onerous than expected, Darcy kept such hopes from the forefront of even his own mind.

## CHAPTER 7

Lydia lay with the duvet pulled up to her chin, her feet poking out from the opposite side. Elizabeth pulled her half of the duvet to her chest. Cool sea air poured in through open windows at either side of the bed. Elizabeth pulled the blanket taut beneath her armpits, folding her hands on her chest as she looked up at the plasterwork ceiling.

"How did you learn this of Mr. Wickham?" Lydia asked.

Elizabeth bit her lower lip. Worse than Mr. Darcy's failed proposal was the fear Lydia would let slip if she learned the truth of Miss Georgiana's near brush with ruination. Mr. Darcy had entrusted Elizabeth with a dangerous secret, and as much as

Elizabeth needed to protect her sister, she could not risk Mr. Darcy's sister in the process.

Elizabeth said, "I was told in confidence. But you must believe I would not impugn Mr. Wickham's character without cause."

"And when did this ruination happen?"

"A year ago."

Elizabeth could almost hear her sister sorting through their acquaintances in her mind. "Was it a friend of Charlotte?" Lydia shook her head. "No, Charlotte would have said something. As would you, had you known before his leaving Hertfordshire.

Elizabeth said, "It does not matter who he attempted to ruin. It matters Mr. Wickham spared no thought for the young lady's reputation. He cared only for his own betterment.

"I suppose you must've heard all this from Lady Catherine de Bourgh?"

As if Elizabeth would take seriously anything Lady Catherine, a woman so enamored of her own importance, said. The same time, better Lydia believed the rumor from Lady Catherine's mouth about an unnamed young woman of her acquaintance, then Mr. Darcy's sister. Elizabeth said, "I cannot say, having given my word..."

"It was Lady Catherine." Lydia sighed, lifting her feet to expose more of them as she let the duvet fall towards her knees. "And you would tell Jane as much if she asked?"

Elizabeth wished Jane had asked. "I have told no one."

"I thank you for telling me whatever it is you have told me. But we cannot take on faith every pearl of wisdom Lady Catherine de Bourgh lays at our feet. Did she not tell mother in a letter she felt Kitty, and even Mary and I ought to still be in the schoolroom? Not to mention the advice on chickens she sent to our father. And she hardly had kind words for you, Lizzy."

Elizabeth well knew Miss Catherine's opinion of the Bennet family. If only Lady Catherine had not followed up to Elizabeth with seven pages of detailed correspondence about the Bennet family's deficiencies and how they might be most properly addressed.

Too late, Elizabeth realized the depth of her mistake. She ought to have denied involvement from Lady Catherine and let Lydia come to some other conclusion about the source of Elizabeth's information. Perhaps Elizabeth could have invented a young woman in town.

Elizabeth said, "Mr. Wickham is not a man we should encourage."

"Well, if Mr. Wickham is only interested in ruining a girl for her fortune, then you have well assured he will have no further interest in us after hearing your tales of our destitution." Lydia grumbled.

Elizabeth can only hope that was the case.

Unlike Jane, who sometimes threw her arm over Elizabeth on the occasions Elizabeth slipped into her sister's bed, Lydia, upon falling asleep, rolled over, her back to Elizabeth, pulling the blanket more tightly to her.

Elizabeth drifted off to sleep with the wind rustling the curtains in an indistinct whisper punctuated by Lydia's snores.

The next day, Lydia said no more of Elizabeth's revelation, but Elizabeth overheard her asking Mrs. Forster more about the officers, a conversation silenced as Elizabeth entered the breakfast nook.

"Shall we bathe this afternoon," Lydia suggested, holding up a slice of buttered toast with a wide smile.

"You are so fond of the water," Mrs. Forster said, shaking her head.

Elizabeth crossed the room and sat down as

Mrs. Forster rang for a servant to bring an additional plate.

"I will teach you to float. It is easier if you take off your bathing dress."

"I am uncertain..." Mrs. Forster murmured. "Your sister wears one and floats well enough."

Elizabeth preferred bathing in the nude, but she disliked the thought of being witnessed from the shore. Also, she needed to model proper behavior for her sister, who in Brighton had succeeded not only in being a flirt but also a hoyden.

Both Elizabeth and Lydia had learned the basics of swimming from an instructional guide Mr. Bennet kept in his study. A gift from Mr. Gardiner, he explained, who had purchased it from a French merchant.

The guide was in French, which Mary could puzzle through and with limited insight, but the drawings were clear. Elizabeth and her sisters had practiced in a small pond near the village until all could float and maneuver, with varying skill, through the water. Lydia had taken to bathing the best, being the youngest and possessed of absolutely no fear. Elizabeth felt herself competent and Jane less so, more because instead of practicing, she worried about her sisters, entreating Lydia to come closer to the shore and avoid thick patches of lilies and other vegetation which might tangle her arms and legs.

Mary had approached the swimming with the same dogged determination she gave the piano and literature, which meant she could float and move her arms and legs in small, splashing strokes that kept her mostly in place. Kitty followed Lydia, though she possessed more caution and hesitated when Jane called her back, something Lydia never did.

"Come, even in the bathing gown you will float this time. You are too tense. That is your greatest trouble."

Mrs. Forster agreed to give it another try, and after eating and changing, the ladies made their way to the bathing area. As they walked along the shore, Elizabeth looked about, pretending to herself she was not hoping to run again into Mr. Darcy.

Elizabeth changed into her bathing gown and slipped out of the bathing machine after her sister.

After allowing the stocky woman to dip her twice, Lydia floated on her own, lying on her back on the surface of the waves which rose and fell in languid swells. Mrs. Forster was nervous about floating unattended, though Lydia had taught her how to keep herself afloat on the water and use her arms and legs to propel herself.

After a few more "lessons" from Lydia, Mrs. Forster said she preferred to stay close to the dipper, "in case my body decides it no longer wishes to float."

Lydia swam out towards the rocks. The tide was out, and whitecaps beat against the near-exposed area with large rocks bared on the surface. Elizabeth, not wishing to see her sister swept away, swam after. The bathing gown grew heavier with every stroke. Saltwater stung Elizabeth's eyes, and she mistimed her breath, inhaling a mouthful of seawater. She coughed, kicking with her legs to remain afloat.

Lydia swam back in three even strokes. "Lizzy, do you need help?"

Elizabeth coughed again. Feeling more and more foolish about insisting on the gown— who would see her so far out?—said, "I am fine."

Lydia stayed until Elizabeth was steady enough to float again.

"You can go back to Mrs. Forster if you like," Lydia offered.

"I dislike you so far out on your own."

"It is more likely I shall need to rescue you than

you me, as you have chosen to bathe in that foolish outfit."

Lydia, calling Elizabeth the fool. Worse, Lydia had the right of it.

After a few more moments, Lydia said, "It is closer to those rocks there than back to the bathing machine. You can rest awhile before returning."

Elizabeth did not like venturing out farther, but it was true the rocks were closer, and Lydia would go on with or without Elizabeth. "Yes," she agreed.

Lydia waved for Elizabeth to follow, and Elizabeth did. After a few more strokes, Lydia laughed and ducked beneath the water, her feet kicking the surface like a mermaid tail.

Just as Elizabeth began to worry, Lydia broke the surface at Elizabeth's side.

Lydia said, "You really ought to shed your gown."

"If I undress here, I may as well throw it away forever."

Lydia wiped water from her eyes. "Just a bit farther. You can tie it about your waist or some such before we return."

Lydia swam ahead, taking a couple of strokes and then looking back to check on Elizabeth.

Elizabeth took a deep breath, held it, and

followed. Lydia scrambled up onto a rock, kneeling and staring out into the exposed sandbank as Elizabeth grabbed ahold. As Elizabeth pulled herself up, the motion making her shoulders feel like lead, made worse by the soggy weight of her bathing dress, Lydia called out, "Look!"

"What?" Elizabeth threw her leg up for better purchase. Gasping, on her knees, she looked to where Lydia pointed. A young seal lay on the sand. Its back fins were caught in a tangle of seaweed. It flopped about, barking in obvious misery.

"We have to help him," Lydia declared as she started down onto the sand towards the seal.

"Wait!" Elizabeth called out. "It might bite."

But Lydia, as normal, ignored her. Elizabeth, both feeling sympathy for the poor animal and also not wishing to see her sister injured, scrambled up and then down the rock to could follow Lydia onto the exposed sandbank.

Elizabeth said, "When the tide comes back in, he will be able to extricate himself."

"That could be hours. And look at him. He's a baby."

As Lydia approached, the seal barked again, flopping and beating its flippers on the ground.

Elizabeth's bathing dress hung heavy from her

shoulders, clinging to her skin in a sopping shroud. She looked behind her to the shoreline. This far out, she and Lydia should not be recognizable, though their nudity would still be obvious.

Lydia knelt beside the seal, talking to it softly. "Just stay still, and we will help you. She knelt to grasp at some of the seaweed which was tangling the seal's back flippers. This close, Elizabeth noticed the seal had been caught in not only seaweed, but also a broken fisherman's net which had broken the skin as the seal struggled.

Poor creature.

Lydia tried to touch his head and the seal, panicked, whipped his head towards Lydia, teeth bared.

"Oh!" Lydia scrambled back.

"He is scared," Elizabeth said. "We need to hold him still." Unfortunately, she only had one idea of how to manage this, and it involved her removing her bathing dress and throwing it over the head of the terrified animal.

With a sigh, Elizabeth knelt, hoping the rocks at least would block the view of her from the shore, and pulled her dress off over her head. She asked, "If I put this over his head and hold him in place, can you untangle his fins?"

"Yes. Lizzy, sometimes you are brilliant!"

Elizabeth sighed, holding her soaked bathing dress out between both hands. "Get behind him," she said. "You see the net. I do not know how long I can hold him."

As it was, she would have to throw the dress over his face and then straddle him. Hopefully the darkness would calm him. It sometimes worked on horses and birds.

Lydia, uncaring of any ogling of her from the shore, crept around the seal to position herself near its back flipper.

As soon as her sister nodded to show she was in place, Elizabeth, gripping the wet frock, threw herself on top of the seal.

The seal was young and relatively small, but even so, with her entire weight atop him, Elizabeth was nearly thrown.

Elizabeth shouted, "Get him free!" as the seal sunk his teeth into the dress an inch below Elizabeth's heel.

Lydia pulled at the net and with a rapid fluttering of fingers began to unravel it.

"Shh, little one." Elizabeth crooned. "Everything will be fine. We just want to help you."

The seal flung his body and tail around, making

Lydia mutter under her breath while Elizabeth sang nonsense notes.

The seal was not impressed. He struggled harder as Lydia pulled the net again and his back flippers came loose. Elizabeth and Lydia jumped back as the seal rolled onto his back, flopped free of Elizabeth's dress as he went around again, righting himself. He laid there, chest heaving, beside Elizabeth's fallen frock. Blood speckled the sand from where the net had dug into the seal's skin, creating a crisscross of fine cuts above his back flipper.

"Maybe if we give him more space," Elizabeth said, taking another step back until her heel, thankfully uninjured, touched the water's edge.

"Go on," Lydia said, waving the seal towards the water. "Go on, Ernest."

Ernest, because of course, Lydia had named the seal, took another breath and wiggling forward again to the water. In one smooth motion, he slid beneath and vanished.

Lydia leapt to her feet, clapping. "We did it, Lizzy! We saved him!" She ran to Elizabeth and hugged her.

Elizabeth, now that the seal and his teeth had left, realized she was shaking. She laughed, noting a ragged edge to her voice. "We did," she said, breathing out a long sigh.

"I had not expected Ernest to become so violent."

"The seal is not a pet, Lydia. He is a wild animal."

"Do you think Ernest will remember how we helped him?"

Elizabeth rather hoped he forgot the whole ordeal. Not wishing to be observed from the shore again, Elizabeth crawled towards her bathing dress. Hopefully, Ernest had not taken too many chunks from it. Elizabeth was tired, and she did not look forward to hauling the garment back to Miss Forster and the bathing machine. Maybe if she tied it around her waist, it might not weigh her down as much.

At least the tide was still out, and she could rest for a few minutes.

Elizabeth balled up the bathing frock so she could rest her head on it and lay down with her back on the sand.

Lydia lay down beside her. "I hope Ernest didn't bite you."

"No, Ernest contented himself with gnawing on the gown."

"I suppose it is fortunate you wore the frock, else we might not have been able to extricate him."

Elizabeth agreed. "Though, should he be caught here again, I will not be wearing it." At this point, what did it matter if Elizabeth swam in the nude? So long as she remained submerged in the water, at least no one on the shore would see her.

Lydia was quiet a moment longer, before she asked, "Do you think, from here, we could swim to where the gentlemen are?""

"Lydia!"

"You must have considered it."

Elizabeth had been more afraid of the gentlemen swimming to them than her doing the opposite. "It must be a mile or further. We would expire. Or at least I would. I am not as adept in the water as you."

"I am glad to be adept at something. At least more adept than yourself."

Surprised at the resentment in her sister's tone, Elizabeth said, "You are wonderful at embroidery and fashion. Far better than myself. I haven't the patience. Without your clever fingers, I suspect Ernest would still be caught."

Lydia sighed. "I suppose. And yet I am silly and you accomplished. More so than Mary, who is proficient at the pianoforte and well versed in the classics."

"It is only because I am older. If you apply yourself with the same diligence, you too can achieve the same accomplishment. Perhaps more."

"I haven't the patience for pianoforte."

Elizabeth, in a moment of common feeling, said, "Neither have I. I enjoy it sometimes, but I haven't Mary's devotion."

Lydia laughed. "I do not believe any of us can manage Mary's devotion to anything Mary devotes herself to. I sometimes wonder if she would be happier to join an order, though she says she wishes a husband and family more than anything."

Elizabeth said, "I wish to marry for love."

"I think I should like to be a widow."

"A widow!" Elizabeth gasped. "You do not wish your husband to live?"

Elizabeth did not think often of her later years, but if she married for love as she wished, she wanted them to have decades together. If one went first, Elizabeth preferred it be herself. Though ideally, both she and her husband would die in the same moment and ascend to heaven together.

How morbid. Elizabeth threw her arms over her eyes to shield her lids from the sun.

Lydia said, "Not that I wish my husband to pass. I am not cruel, and I think I should enjoy being married and having a baby. Only, it seems widows are not so constrained by what is proper. In Papa's Morning Post, I read a widow has opened her own shop in London. I should love to make designs and have a shop, not that I should well understand how one buys such things. I asked our aunt. It was years ago, but she said a dressmaker's life is a drudgery, and I should look towards marriage and charity work."

Of course, Elizabeth knew her sister had interests. When Lydia was younger, while she did not take to painting, she had always enjoyed looking through fashion plates and drawing imitations of the clothing. She also had a wonderful eye for color. Because Lydia's interests had been so specific, and her hand and eye for landscapes uninspired, none had thought to consider her doodles of serious interest. But if Lydia had asked her aunt about opening a shop, then there had been more than a passing fancy.

Lydia said, "You do not have to look so surprised, Lizzy. I know Papa thinks me silly as I have never had much interest in reading. At least not of the reading that would lead to my betterment, as our cousin would say, but I have thought of things beyond assemblies and handsome men."

Elizabeth felt shame. "If I can help you open a shop, I will," she said.

But Lydia laughed. "No! Our aunt was correct. A shop is a drudgery. Why the ladies engage in work from dawn into the dark, and they hardly walk outside. It gives you a squint, and your fingers curl. Not to mention the horrific number of pinpricks.

"No, I do not need a shop. Perhaps an iron-works, if I can find a strong man to be my partner. I cannot marry a man in trade, but perhaps if he is an officer with a large stipend, there might be some allowance? The second or third son of a baronet perhaps. That would be acceptable. He would also need funds."

Elizabeth rubbed her fingers over her eyes. She sat up. "Perhaps we should start back."

Lydia said, "Best we tie the net up in your dress. I would not want Ernest or any of his friends to be caught in it again. They may not have us around to swim out and save them."

A sensible plan. Though after the garment had been gnawed on by a seal and wrapped around a dirty, seaweed stained net, Elizabeth might be better to do as Lydia had suggested and leave it here.

They swam together, with Lydia most often dragging the soaking wet bundle of dress and net. Mrs. Forster had already climbed back into the bathing machine when they arrived. She poked her head out from the modesty curtain, calling to them, "Why did you swim out so far? What happened? Lydia, when you stood, the sun was behind you but from your shadow it was clear you wore not a stitch."

Lydia retold the story of their rescue, and Mrs. Forster listened with rapt attention as they changed.

Upon looking at Elizabeth's seaweed-stained bathing gown, Mrs. Forster shook her head. "I shall have my maid see what she can do, but I fear it is a loss, Lizzy."

Elizabeth was least concerned about the dress. "Better it than me. That seal had sharp teeth." She held up the gnawed, ripped section.

"Oh, my!" Mrs. Forster put her hand to her mouth. "Miss Elizabeth Bennet, you must be more careful."

Elizabeth smothered a sigh. She was not the one who insisted on rescuing 'Ernest,' after swimming out too far from shore.

"But tonight, we shall put all thoughts of drowning behind us. My husband says we shall have more officers tonight. They have transferred a new group in. Is that not grand, Lydia?"

Lydia smiled. "Wonderful!"

Elizabeth sighed. At least a crop of new and handsome officers would distract Lydia from Mr. Wickham.

# CHAPTER 8

The next morning, Mr. Darcy wrote to his solicitor to see what he could unearth about Baron Dunham's financial situation. Bingley rose late, as usual, and Darcy had finished his breakfast, his letter, and was well through the first half of the Brighton Gazette when his friend knocked.

It was half ten, and Darcy was dressed for the afternoon. This early, Darcy expected his friend to still be in his morning dress and slippers, but he too wore breeches, a day jacket and loose-fitting shirt if no cravat.

Bingley grinned, waving Darcy towards him. "You have already eaten, have you? Well, join me for breakfast anyway. I smell sausages from the common room."

So that was why Bingley had dressed.

"They can be brought here," Darcy said. He had kept his breakfast light—eggs and buttered toast—but Bingley would want something more substantial. And of course he would prefer to dine where he could meet and greet the hotel's other guests.

"Darcy, you must get out more. Besides, Louisa says Mr. Dunham often happens upon my sister in the common breakfast room, and I should like to be there to chaperone should I need be. Louisa asked me."

"I thought Mr. Dunham was supervising his renovations."

"In the early morning, but it seems he leaves them to their devices for some part of the day." Bingley shrugged. "Come on now. I know how you hate mingling with the common masses."

"It is not that," Darcy said, remembering Miss Elizabeth's admonishments of his behavior to those he considered 'beneath' him. Worse, there was some truth to Miss Elizabeth's statements. He was the nephew of an earl and the master of an important estate. And he sounded like a proper arse even as he laid out the arguments in his own mind. He disliked strangers and idle conversation. But Bingley was his friend, and Darcy owed him. Smothering a sigh, Darcy rose. "Let me get my paper."

He folded it along its ironed crease and followed Bingley from his room, down the stairs and into the common room.

Thankfully, the room was not crowded. Three large tables and a smattering of smaller ones were arranged about the pleasant room, which had all of its windows open to the brisk sea-air. The smell of sausages mingled with salt, and though Darcy had already eaten, his stomach rumbled.

Bingley offered cheerful greetings to the smattering of patrons already seated: an old man, crumbs flecking his beard, muttering to himself while scribbling in a notebook, a pair of middle-aged ladies and a girl of twelve whose cheek's reddened as Bingley offered the trio a pleasant hello.

When they finally sat, Darcy felt like he had been scrubbed with sand. But he maintained his gentlemanly manners, smiling at and bowing to all he passed, joining Bingley in giving his opinion of the day's weather, though it was far too early in the day to engage in such pleasantries.

VIOLET KING

"You are in a pleasant mood this morning," Bingley remarked as they sat.

"Am I?"

"Well, you have always been most irritatingly coherent before noon," Bingley said with a laugh. "You were up with the sun today, I suspect."

"Not so early," Darcy said. "The sun was well risen at half seven."

"Half seven!" Bingley shook his head with a laugh. "Scandalous. You realize we have an assembly this evening, and the ladies should like it if you were awake to the second set of dances."

"I have been informed a dance requires some interest in idle conversation, which I possess little talent for and less interest. So I suspect they shall not mind my absence."

A servant arrived with two plates full of eggs, potatoes and sausages. Bingley tucked into his with an appreciative noise. Darcy, less inclined towards idle conversation, remained silent.

Bingley laughed. "How do you like him? Mr. Dunham. I admit, I am not so fond of travel by sea. It is dangerous with changes in weather and water all around."

Darcy asked, "You cannot swim?"

"Where might I have gained such a skill?" Bingley's eyes narrowed. "You can. How did you learn?"

"My father's valet. He taught Wickham and myself. His father was a naval man."

"I thought naval men were superstitious about swimming. They say it causes ships to sink."

Darcy shrugged. "Mr. Montrose said that was as his father believed, and then his ship sank, and he was carried to the bottom within a half-mile of shore. I do not know where Mr. Montrose learned, but he insisted we learn. My father as well. Though my father did not take to it. We learned at the seaside, well north of here. The water was frigid, but after a while, I enjoyed it."

"Bathing is pleasant enough, but boats…" Bingley shook his head. "The rocking makes me ill. I do not know how to tell my sister, but I fear I may not be able to chaperone. I will spend the time puking over the deck. I have thought of it the entire night. But if you have no such troubles with seasickness, then perhaps you and Louisa can go together, and I can claim some illness. It is close to the truth as I will certainly be ill should I join you on this excursion."

Chaperoning Miss Bingley to meet and socialize with yet another group of strangers was not Darcy's idea of a pleasant evening, but again, he owed his friend. "If you need me, I shall go."

"Excellent. I cannot thank you enough, Darcy. You are a true friend."

Guilt squeezed Darcy's guts. He said, "If your sister and Mr. Dunham are as well-suited to each other as it seems, and Mrs. Hurst's fears prove unfounded, then I know you shall be made quite glad."

Bingley cut another piece of sausage and popped it into his mouth. "If only I could have such happiness. You will say I am the sort of man enamored with the *idea* of love, but..."

Darcy asked, "Do you still think of her?"

Bingley averted his gaze, and asked, "Miss Bennet? How could I? It has been months and months, and Miss Jane Bennet is not thinking of me. It is as you said. She has found another man of fortune to capture her interest. I doubt she thinks of me at all."

It was on the tip of Darcy's tongue to reveal Miss Elizabeth's assertion that her sister was heartbroken. But to say that, Darcy would also have to reveal his own declaration, and Miss Elizabeth's flat rejection of it.

Darcy could not risk losing his friend's good

opinion without being sure of Miss Bennet's affection.

So what if his obstinacy made him a coward and a liar.

And then there was the issue of Miss Elizabeth Bennet and her sister Miss Lydia. Both would attend this evening's assembly. Darcy at the least had to tell his friend of their meeting yesterday on the shore. If Bingley found out from the other ladies, it would only compound the wrong Mr. Darcy may have already committed.

Darcy said, "Miss Elizabeth and Miss Lydia Bennet are here. In Brighton."

Bingley put his fork onto the plate. "Where? Here?" he asked, glancing around him. "At the hotel?"

Darcy shook his head. "No, they are holiday here with…" Mr. Darcy did not know Mrs. Forster's relationship to the Bennets. "I happened upon them last night, before dinner."

"And you've waited so long to tell me," Bingley said. "Is Miss Jane here?"

"No."

Bingley sighed. "I suppose it does not matter. She was not enamored of me. Merely being polite, as you said. Or perhaps following her mother's whim." Bingley laughed, a hollow, bitter sound. "At least I do not have to have that woman as my mother by marriage. I should wish to throw myself into the sea, or from my carriage while in motion, if that became the case.

Darcy said, "Miss Elizabeth and Miss Lydia should be at tonight's assembly."

"And we must go. It had been my intention, and now— Perhaps we should not. Perhaps it would be better if we stayed. Except, my sister. No, we must go."

Darcy said, "I can go in your stead."

Bingley sawed at his sausage. "I cannot ask that of you. For one, I know you are not fond of crowds of strangers. You will stand behind my sister and glower, which will make her new suitor believe you are harboring affection. You are not harboring affection for Caroline, are you?"

"No."

"No…" Bingley sighed. "I had not thought so. It would be nice to call you a brother in truth, as opposed to merely of the heart, but we cannot control such things.

Darcy said, "It is possible my initial concerns about Miss Jane Bennet were overdrawn."

"Nonsense!" Bingley said. He took a bite of his

eggs, chewed, and swallowed. "I saw the truth as well as you, when you forced me to look past my infatuation. Miss Bennet never showed me special affection. She was, as you said, practicing good manners."

Darcy could not leave his friend in ignorance, especially not with Miss Elizabeth in Brighton. If they crossed paths, Miss Elizabeth would tell Bingley the truth of her sister's heartbreak.

Perhaps that would be for the best. Let Miss Elizabeth make the case for her sister. Except, in deference to Darcy's original warning, Bingley would not give Miss Elizabeth a fair hearing. And if Darcy was wrong, he owed his friend the truth. It was a matter of honor.

Darcy leaned towards his friend, "Bingley, I have something I must—"

"Charles?"

Darcy and Bingley looked up from their meal. Miss Bingley was in her walking dress, complete with a parasol, which tapped the ground as she made the final three steps towards Darcy and Bingley's table.

Both men stood. Darcy bowed. Charles said, "Caroline? What is it?"

"We need to speak. What is it you wrote about

not joining us for tomorrow's outing with Mr. Dunham?"

"I did not say I wouldn't, but you know how I am about boats," Bingley said. "Have you eaten? We can call a servant to bring you a chair."

"I had breakfast in my rooms with Louisa," Miss Bingley said, but she waved to a servant. "I can have chocolate though." From staying with the Bingley's at Netherfield, Darcy knew well Miss Bingley's love of chocolate. "Now what is it you were saying to my brother, Mr. Darcy?"

"It was nothing," Darcy said. Hard enough to reveal his shame to Bingley. He would be a fool to speak of Miss Bennet in the presence of Bingley's gossiping sister.

"Men's business, then," Miss Bingley said with a laugh. A servant approached, carrying a chair. Miss Bingley sat. "Now, Mr. Dunham says there is nothing to fear. His yacht is large and cuts through the water smoothly..."

Later, Darcy decided. He would tell his friend everything later. Despite Darcy's good intentions, he could not help but feel gratitude at Miss Bingley for offering Darcy a reprieve from his own conscience.

At least for now.

## CHAPTER 9

Despite Mrs. Forster's hinting that they leave early for the assembly, before "the eligible gentlemen are already engaged with other ladies," Lydia's insistence upon changing three times meant it was near eleven before she, Elizabeth, and Mrs. Forster arrived. Elizabeth glanced over the hall, caught between relief and disappointment at Mr. Darcy's absence. Not that she had expected Mr. Darcy to subject himself to an assembly with the common masses, no matter his polite agreement days earlier.

Elizabeth's gaze fell on the young officer from the previous night's dinner. He was speaking with another gentleman, but Mr. Stewart's body and a group of other ladies, obscured Elizabeth's view of him. She leaned closer to Lydia, who walked with her arm linked with Miss Forster and chattering wildly. "There is Mr. Stewart! He seems..." Elizabeth's breath caught as Mr. Stewart turned, his gaze caught by something on the refreshments table, and Elizabeth realized the gentleman he was speaking with was Mr. Wickham.

Lydia looked up. "Mr. Stewart? This is the third time you have mentioned him since last night. Are you forming an attachment?" Lydia's eyes sparkled, and Elizabeth knew her sister jested. Unfortunately, Mrs. Forster took her friend's words with apparent sincerity. "Are you? I had thought Mr. Stewart a touch young, but affection knows no age. He is likely to be quick on his feet, I suppose. Shall we approach him?"

"No." The last thing Elizabeth wished was to engage in a conversation, however tangentially, with Mr. Wickham. And she could not risk putting Lydia in Wickham's path again.

"Have courage!" Mrs. Forster said with a smile. "We shall speak with him together. Then you will show no sign of favoritism or impropriety."

Before Elizabeth could make another protest, Lydia linked her free arm about Elizabeth's elbow and gave it a tug. "Yes, come, Lizzy. Mr. Stewart's conversation will be a delight!"

Once again, Elizabeth wanted to strangle her sister.

With Lydia's hand gripping the top Elizabeth's own, Elizabeth could not extricate herself without causing a scene. Resigned, she followed.

As they approached, Mr. Stewart, eyes wide and cheeks flushed, bowed. "Miss Bennet! Miss Lydia! Mrs. Forster! It is a pleasure to see you again."

Elizabeth took a breath. Mr. Stewart's excitement only added to Elizabeth's trepidation. Perhaps she should take her mother's lead and claim a sudden onslaught of anxiety. *"Oh, my nerves!"* But Elizabeth could not bring herself to such silliness. Besides, a part of her feared Mr. Darcy discovering Elizabeth's sudden change in character. The man had made his opinion of Elizabeth's family clear, and Elizabeth should give no thought to his regard, but she did.

Hopefully she could keep this conversation with Mr. Wickham brief. She had already endured too much of his company at Mrs. Forster's dinner.

Mr. Wickham bowed and said, in a more measured tone, "It is a pleasure to see the three of you this evening. I suppose my wish to dance will be met with disappointment as three ladies as lovely as yourselves must already have filled your dance cards?"

Mrs. Forster said, "Oh, no! We have just arrived. I am certain there is a space on all of our cards for a dance."

"Yes!" Lydia added.

Blast! There was no polite way to refuse Mr. Wickham after Mrs. Forster had accepted for the three of them. And Lydia, knowing of Mr. Wickham's history, still put herself in Mr. Wickham's path. It was infuriating. Elizabeth debated feigning a headache or exhaustion to refuse Mr. Wickham, but her father had charged her with keeping Lydia out of trouble. An increasingly difficult task.

Elizabeth handed her dance card to Mr. Stewart and said, "I enjoy dancing. It gives me pleasure to fill my card with a variety of partners." It was the closest she could come to refusing Mr. Wickham without saying as much.

Mr. Stewart signed his name as Lydia giggled with Mr. Wickham. When Mr. Wickham turned to Elizabeth and said, "Miss Bennet. It is a pleasant surprise to see you and your sister tonight."

"Hardly a surprise," Elizabeth said. "Considering we sat across from each other just yesterday at Mrs. Forster's dinner."

"Touché. I ought not to have forgotten your wit or facility at observation in our time apart."

Their time apart. Mr. Wickham spoke as though there had been something between them. Elizabeth's stomach churned. "I am certain you have had much to occupy you since your brief visit to Hertfordshire."

"I trust time has not eroded your good opinion of me, Miss Bennet."

Elizabeth forced a laugh. "Whenever did I say I had a good opinion of you?"

Mr. Wickham, his lips upturned in an edged smile, said, "At least allow me one dance to give opportunity to change a lady's impression."

Before Elizabeth could demur, Lydia took the dance card from Elizabeth's hand and said, "Do not mind my sister's jests. Lizzy is a prickly fruit, our mama sometimes says."

It was all Elizabeth could do to maintain her placid expression.

"The prickliest fruits bear the sweetest juice." Mr. Wickham jotted his name and handed the card back to Elizabeth. His handwriting was elegant, a gentleman's hand, and Elizabeth, knowing it, like the rest of him, a fraud, resented the even flourish of his script.

Mr. Wickham's gloved hand lingered, brushing over the top of Elizabeth's as the next set of guests was announced.

Mr. and Miss Bingley, and Mr. Darcy and Mrs. Hurst. And a Mr. Dunham.

Mr. Wickham gave a start when he heard Mr. Darcy's name. He looked towards the doorway, his face losing color as he looked over the new arrivals.

Considering Mr. Wickham and Mr. Darcy's history, Elizabeth expected Mr. Wickham to bow and scurry off, but his gaze remained fixed on them. Not them, the third man. What was his name? Mr. Dunham?

Lydia said, "Oh! Is that Miss Caroline Bingley, and who is the handsome man on her arm?"

She fluttered her eyelashes at Mr. Stewart who blushed and stuttered, "He is Baron Dunham's eldest son."

"What a lovely couple they make. And I see Mr. Bingley has no Miss on his arm." Lydia glanced back at Elizabeth. "Perhaps he has not found another love."

"We do not know if Mr. Bingley has found a first

love, let alone another," Elizabeth said with some acid. As furious as she was at Mr. Darcy for turning Mr. Bingley away from Jane, Mr. Bingley himself shared some responsibility. Perhaps it had only been an infatuation on his part. He seemed amiable enough, now. A man who traveled to Brighton to amuse himself was not one in the throes of heartbreak.

She glanced at Mr. Darcy who stepped into the hall after Mr. Bingley. His gaze drifted over the assembly, as though he was looking for something. Or someone. Elizabeth resisted the urge to step away from Wickham, but she angled her body away from the man, who took that moment to lean in and whisper, "It surprises me to see Mr. Darcy mingling with such as us."

Elizabeth said, "I do not see him mingling with anybody."

Mr. Wickham laughed, and Elizabeth hated it. Worse, Mr. Darcy, in that moment froze, his gaze fixed on her.

Mr. Bingley leaned towards his friend, whispering something with obvious concern. Then, Mr. Bingley followed Mr. Darcy's gaze.

"Miss Bennet?" Mr. Stewart said. "Are you well?"

"Quite." Elizabeth curtsied. "I look forward to our dance."

Mr. Stewart flushed again and said, "Yes. I look forward to it." He looked at Mr. Wickham. "Any man looks forward to dancing with a lady so... accomplished... as yourself. As yourselves."

Elizabeth smothered a laugh. She did not wish to upset the poor man, though he did not know of Elizabeth or Lydia's accomplishments beyond their ability to don a gown and cut their meat, chew and swallow it without choking. Mr. Stewart had a less demanding view of accomplishment than Mr. Darcy, who only knew of four women who had managed the feat.

Had Mr. Darcy's proposal indicated Elizabeth was the fifth?

Why was she allowing his proposal to affect her so? She had rejected Mr. Collins with little thought thereafter.

Perhaps it was how he had seemed so solicitous, walking with Lydia and Mrs. Forster along the shore. Or perhaps it was his letter. Knowing him capable of emotions beyond arrogance and disdain, she could appreciate the handsome sweep of his jaw and how well his breeches showed the curve of his muscular thighs and calves, only partially obscured by his gleaming Hessians.

Elizabeth remembered Mr. Darcy's scent, the hint of sandalwood mixing with the salt sea air.

All of this remembering was futile. Elizabeth had proclaimed him the last man she would ever consider marrying, and after so firm a rejection, she could not hope to capture his interest again. Why would she want to? Yes, she might have been wrong about Mr. Wickham, but the rest of it still applied. Mr. Darcy had still inserted himself between Jane and Mr. Bingley. And Mr. Bingley's holiday here made it clear Mr. Darcy had been unwilling or unable to rectify the situation.

Lydia smiled, and once again abandoning all propriety, gave Mr. Bingley a bright wave.

"Lydia!" Elizabeth snapped.

"We are acquainted. This is not London where you have to watch your every step and smile. Come, let us offer our greetings to Miss Bingley. I imagine nothing improper in that."

As much as Lydia irritated Elizabeth, she could not deny, despite all reason, she still wished to speak with Mr. Darcy again, if only to explain she had spoken to Mr. Wickham only from politeness.

Though Mr. Wickham's flourishing signature on

Elizabeth's dance card would make a lie of her explanations.

Lydia strode forward, and Elizabeth, Mr. Stewart, and Mrs. Forster followed.

"Excuse me," Mr. Wickham said as they left, remaining behind.

The musicians, a cellist, a violinist, and a young man on the piano, began tuning their instruments. The dancing would start shortly. Elizabeth did not wish to dance. Especially not with Mr. Wickham. It was unlikely Mr. Darcy would sign her dance card, and a dance with Mr. Bingley would be awkward at best.

Blast Mr. Wickham and Mr. Darcy for further complicating Elizabeth's life yet again!

Miss Bingley and Mr. Dunham stood close to the refreshments table, at the opposite end of the semicircle with Mr. Bingley, Mrs. Hurst, and Mr. Darcy at the opposite end. As Lydia, Elizabeth, and Mrs. Forster approached, Mr. Dunham gestured to the table and bowed to the others, presumably to bring glasses of Ratafia for Miss Bingley and Mrs. Hurst.

Miss Bingley gave Elizabeth and Lydia a tight smile as the three approached. "Miss Lydia. Miss Elizabeth. I suppose your sister, Miss Bennet, is otherwise occupied?"

Lydia said, "My sister Jane was not well enough to join us, but I will tell her you asked after her."

Miss Bingley turned towards Mrs. Forster. "I have not had the pleasure of your acquaintance."

"Mrs. Amelia Forster," Elizabeth said, holding out her hand toward the woman, who curtsied. "We are her guests."

Miss Bingley returned the gesture, lowering herself to the barest requirements of courtesy.

"Miss Bennet is ill?" Mr. Bingley asked, his brows lowering. "I hope it is nothing serious."

"Miss Bennet, poor dear, is often ill at inconvenient moments, it seems."

Elizabeth's neck tightened. She said, "Jane would never wish to inconvenience anyone. I fear she is more susceptible to shocks than most. A sudden storm. A surprising chill. The sense of abandonment. My sister's kindness has imposed upon her an aggressive sensitivity."

"Something inherited from her mother, I suppose..." Miss Bingley mused.

"From our father. He endures excitements, hiding behind a placid and sometimes joking demeanor that which causes him heartbreak. But you and I are different sorts, I suspect. We speak our minds when the situation warrants."

Miss Bingley's eyes narrowed. "Heartbreak?"

Elizabeth laughed. "Let us not speak of melancholy things. My sister would not wish to cause anyone an inconvenience."

"But, heartbreak?" Mr. Bingley asked. "Has she—?"

Miss Bingley snapped, "Miss Elizabeth was speaking of her father. Miss Bennet is merely ill. As seems common to one of her...delicate constitution."

"My sister does not suffer a delicate constitution!" Lydia protested. "She nurses each of us through our illnesses."

Mr. Darcy said, "Miss Bennet always showed care for the sensibilities of others, and her sisters' devotion is but evidence of the young lady's kind nature."

Mr. Bingley's eyes widened as he turned to his friend. "Truly? You never spoke so highly of Miss Bennet before."

"An error," Mr. Darcy said. "I had hoped—"

"Miss Bingley, Mrs. Hurst," Mr. Dunham returned, a glass of Ratafia in each hand. He bowed, handing his leftmost glass first to Mrs. Hurst and the second to Miss Bingley. Their fingers—gloved, of course—touched, his thumb against the pad of her middle finger as his index finger brushed below her pulse, where her thumb met her wrist. Their gazes locked, and Miss Bingley, breathless, thanked him.

"It is my pleasure. I imagine, sometimes, I should like to be a knight of old, offering my deepest service for the scent of a lady's handkerchief and the fleeting beauty of her smile."

Mrs. Hurst's lips pursed at the man's gallantry, and Mr. Darcy, eyes narrowed, kept his gaze fixed upon Mr. Dunham's expression. Elizabeth could not fathom why. Perhaps Mr. Darcy was a man who hated to see anyone else happy?

Mr. Darcy had written he had interfered between Mr. Bingley and Jane to protect his friend, but Mr. Darcy's drive to protect drove others away. Until the moment of his proposal, Elizabeth had not thought Mr. Darcy felt disapprobation towards her, and perhaps a certain fascination, but not love. Certainly not the ardent love he had declared in insults, each stacked upon the last.

Mr. Darcy had no business advising anyone in their relationships.

And yet, something about Mr. Dunham's praise

put Elizabeth on edge. Maybe it was because she had been so quick to fall for Mr. Wickham's solicitude. A woman was susceptible to one who expressed agreement with her own opinions. And who held herself in a higher regard than Miss Caroline Bingley?

Miss Bingley said, "If ever there was a man who showed an understanding of chivalry, I should lay handkerchief to brow and proclaim you him."

Mr. Dunham smiled.

Elizabeth smothered a sigh. The treacle of their conversation turned her stomach. Perhaps it was she who could not bear seeing another happy.

Miss Bingley said, "The first space on my dance card is not yet filled."

"I should not like the first, but the seventh. There is a new dance, from the continent, the Regent has introduced...."

Mrs. Forster said, "The waltz! They say it is scandalous!"

"I have heard nothing of this dance," Mr. Bingley said, cocking his head.

Mrs. Forster brushed the front of her frock with her palm. "It is from France."

"We are at war with France," Mr. Darcy said.

"We are at war with Napoleon," Lydia said.

"I have not had the courage to try it," Mr. Dunham said, glancing downward at his and Miss Bingley's hands, cradling the glass. "Perhaps it is best I take another dance."

"No!" Miss Bingley said. "Let us try. You, Mr. Dunham, of all people, would not dare take advantage. This is a public assembly. They would allow nothing truly indecent."

Elizabeth glanced at her dance card, noting with relief Mr. Wickham had taken the fourth and not the seventh dance.

Lydia glanced at her card, her cheeks coloring. "It seems my seventh is already filled."

"By who?" Elizabeth reached for the card, fearing Mr. Wickham's name was beside that number, but Lydia pulled the card away, holding it against her opposite hip, face down. "Mrs. Forster is our chaperone, not you. And she has deemed it very acceptable."

Mrs. Forster bit her bottom lip and nodded. "There is no harm in dancing. So long as one does not accept a second in the same evening, of course."

Lydia laughed. "With so many fine gentlemen, I should be grateful to find a place on my card for each of them, no matter the dance."

"I shall see if Mr. Forster is available. He does not enjoy dancing, but if I inform him I may try *this* dance with another..."

"And you, Miss Bennet?" Mr. Bingley asked.

Elizabeth tensed in horror at the thought of Mr. Bingley asking her to dance, especially a dance considered scandalous.

"I think I should prefer to observe as I am unfamiliar with the steps."

"It is a simple, one-two-three," Lydia said, stepping up and around in a triangular motion. "Mrs. Forster showed me this afternoon. Do you see?"

Mr. Darcy said, "We shall observe." He took a step closer to Elizabeth. Because he wanted to protect her from scandal or found her too inclined to relish it?

What would it be like to engage in a scandalous dance with Mr. Darcy?

Lydia laughed. "Lizzy would say that. She is so very proper. You are well suited."

Elizabeth's fingers twitched.

Lydia added, "I see you have not yet asked my sister to dance."

Blast her sister. Elizabeth had already rejected Mr. Darcy's proposal. Now Lydia was putting the man in a most embarrassing position. Worse, if

Elizabeth showed her dance card, he would see Mr. Wickham's name signed upon it and feel she had ignored his letter and was engaging in a flirtation.

"I apologize. My sister is too forward," Elizabeth said.

"A gentleman would not wish to put himself in a position where his attentions were unwelcome."

"I did not say they were unwelcome."

Mr. Darcy cocked his head. "Perhaps I was mistaken?"

Elizabeth said, "Both my sister and I have room. For a dance."

"I see."

Yes, Elizabeth would strangle Lydia in their shared bed this evening. A hanging for murder was preferable to this mortification. At least it would end in one horrid moment instead of through this series of tiny cuts.

"I apologize," Elizabeth said.

"May I?"

"What?"

"Your dance card." Mr. Darcy held out his hand, and mutely, Elizabeth handed it over. His gaze narrowed as he looked over the signatures. "I see you and Mr. Wickham are still acquainted."

"Distantly," Elizabeth said. "There are proprieties to observe."

"I had not thought you one to indulge in proprieties when offering a refusal," Mr. Darcy said.

Elizabeth flinched. She did not mean to, but his words were a slap. She said, "If you do not wish to dance—"

"I wish to dance," Mr. Darcy said and wrote his name in the sixth position. "And Miss Lydia?"

The musicians, who had been running through a series warm-up notes, stopped, and the first dance was announced.

CHAPTER 10

D arcy seethed. Had he not warned Miss Elizabeth about Mr. Wickham? At least she had the grace to look embarrassed.

He had been a fool to accept Miss Elizabeth's invitation to dance. Or more accurately, her sister's invitation. Miss Elizabeth had made her disdain for him clear, and he was a fool to have expected his letter to change her opinion.

Miss Lydia held her card in her palm and smiled, her cheeks dimpling. "Only if you promise to speak with me."

Of course, Miss Elizabeth had gossiped to her sister's about their dance at Netherfield. But Mr. Darcy, remembering his manners, nodded. "May I?" he asked and held out his hand.

Lydia rocked forward on her feet slightly and held the card out. Wickham's name was written there, for the fifth dance.

Surely Miss Elizabeth would not put her sister in such peril out of politeness?

No, Miss Elizabeth had clearly warned her sister. Just as clearly, Miss Lydia had ignored her, feeling Miss Elizabeth too serious. Darcy thought of the fiery, laughing woman who had rejected his proposal. Serious was not a word he would use to describe her.

"Miss Bennet?" A coltish young man in officer red bowed to Miss Elizabeth.

"Mr. Stewart," Miss Elizabeth said. Darcy recognized the name from her dance card. He held out his arm, and she took it, "Shall we?"

The man nodded, his eyes wide. Smitten. Darcy pitied him. Worse, he pitied himself for still wanting her.

Darcy led Lydia to the dance floor. They took their places, three other couples separating them from Miss Elizabeth and Mr. Stewart. The music began, and they took three steps towards each other and clasped hands.

Mr. Darcy said, "I see Mr. Wickham has claimed the privilege of your fifth dance."

Lydia laughed. "And it has Lizzy so mad. She is only here because she fears for my virtue."

Darcy and Lydia circled each other as they spoke. Darcy said, "Perhaps she has reason."

Lydia's eyes widened as Darcy released her hands, and following the steps of the dance, moved away.

When they came together again, Lydia said, "I am not so silly as Lizzy seems to think. She treats me like a child."

Perhaps because Elizabeth's youngest sister acted like a child, but the Darcy had enough sense not to say that aloud.

A fortnight before Wickham had lured Georgiana from Pemberley, Darcy had suspected the girl had some infatuation. He had assumed it was with one of the local tenant's boys or the stableman's son, who was handsome and rumored to be a bit of a buck in the local village.

Georgiana had answered Darcy's questions in a similar tone. "No, there's nothing you should worry about. I have no interest in Jeremy for any of the boys in the village."

They stepped away again, crossing to opposite corners, linking hands of the second partner, a young woman who smiled at Mr. Darcy and asked, "Is this your first assembly in Brighton?"

Darcy agreed, and endured small talk before the dance separated them, and he returned to take Miss Lydia's hands. "Your sister cares for you and does not wish you to spoil your prospects for a bright future," Darcy explained.

"I know that, but when we were young, Lizzy used to be fun. She grew more serious upon coming out, but I think Charlotte's marriage really troubled her. Lizzy has always wished to marry for love, you see, and she thought Charlotte felt the same. But then Charlotte married Mr. Collins, for whom I cannot imagine any woman having a grand passion. I think Lizzy fears the same fate for herself."

Darcy reeled from Miss Lydia's words, and he was grateful the dance carried him away again.

When Miss Elizabeth had said Darcy was the last man she would ever consider marrying, he had thought her reasoning came more from loyalty to her sister and misplaced trust in Mr. Wickham, who was adept at gaining and abusing the trust of all around him. But to discover she wished only to marry for love and found his declaration of it so despicable, so unworthy, made him question his actions since arriving in Brighton.

Yes, Darcy owed it to Bingley to rectify the mistake he had made regarding Miss Jane Bennet. But why keep torturing himself so, thinking of her, dreaming of her, speaking with her, and even insisting upon a dance she had not offered?

The next steps of the dance moved him to a third partner, and to Darcy's dismay, it was Miss Elizabeth. She smiled, dark eyes glittering. "Mr. Darcy," she said. "I hope my sister has not chattered your ear off."

"Her conversation was most edifying."

"I would not take too much from her words. Lydia can be…headstrong."

"She believes you heartbroken since Mrs. Collins' marriage to your cousin."

Miss Elizabeth laughed, but the sound was forced, and she did not meet his eyes. "Surely she does not believe me pining for Mr. Collins? I assure you, I am not."

Darcy could not help but smile in return. "Those were not her exact words."

"I warned Lydia." Elizabeth said. "But she does not believe me."

"She doubts my word?"

"I spoke in generalities," Elizabeth explained, and the dance took them away again.

Was Miss Elizabeth protecting him? Likely she was protecting Georgiana, for which Darcy was grateful. After conversing with Miss Lydia, Darcy would not trust the young woman with a secret. Miss Elizabeth must have felt the same.

Blast! He did not wish to soften to her again. How was it the memory of her lavender scent lingered even as they crossed to opposite sides of the floor?

After a turn and five steps, Darcy took Miss Lydia's hands. "Your sister is serious because she cares for you," he said.

"Do you care for her?" Lydia asked.

"I do." And he was a fool for it. The worst kind of fool, one who did not learn from his own mistakes.

Lydia said, "Then you should tell her."

A final circling, a step back and then together, and the music stopped.

Mr. Darcy bowed.

Lydia smiled and curtsied. "Thank you for a wonderful dance," she said. She leaned in a little closer and said, "I think if you were to tell my sister, you might have a pleasant surprise."

Miss Lydia did not know her sister as well as she thought.

"Or a most unpleasant one," Darcy said bitterly.

"Lydia!" Miss Elizabeth strode towards them. Her shoulders tensed as her gaze flitted between her sister and him.

Darcy bowed to her. "Your sister was simply thanking me for a pleasant dance."

Miss Elizabeth smiled, and Darcy could not tear his eyes away. What was it about her that compelled him so, even now?

"Thank you for the dance and conversation," Darcy said.

He turned away as Miss Lydia leaned towards her sister and whispered something.

Miss Elizabeth hissed back, "Lydia!"

Miss Lydia laughed.

Darcy made his way to the refreshment table. He spooned himself a glass of punch, and sipped it, heedless of the flavor. No more longing for that which he could not have. Miss Elizabeth had rejected him firmly. Darcy would not risk his heart again.

Darcy had promised Bingley he would give his best assessment of Mr. Dunham, and he had promised Mrs. Hurst the same. Instead of pining, he would remember why he was here. Darcy looked over the assembly for Miss Caroline Bingley. She, her brother and her sister stood together at a second table on the opposite side of the room, speaking with another young woman in a lavender gown.

As she had at various events since they were leaving Netherfield, Miss Bingley seemed to encourage a dialogue between her brother and the third woman.

Bingley had remarked on it with rueful acceptance. "I am not inclined towards a bachelor's life, and I know Caroline is trying to help, but her efforts are exhausting, sometimes."

But where was Mr. Dunham? He had been playing court to Miss Bingley most of the evening. But as Darcy looked over the room, he did not see Miss Bingley's most aggressive suitor.

Perhaps he had taken a moment to relieve himself. Darcy put down his glass and left the hall. If he could speak with Mr. Dunham alone, he might get a better understanding of the other man's character.

But as he approached the hallway to the washrooms, Darcy was met with the most upsetting sight. Mr. Wickham and Mr. Dunham stood together, whispering.

Mr. Darcy was grateful for the strip of

carpeting along the floor that muffled the ring of his boots against the flooring. The two men stood close to the wall, Mr. Wickham's back to Darcy, and Mr. Dunham's view partially obscured by a large vase.

Darcy froze, hunching in on himself with the hope the vase was enough to obscure him from view a while longer. He was too far to hear what the two men were saying, but Mr. Wickham reached inside his coat and passed a folded piece of foolscap to the other man. Mr. Dunham slipped it into his coat and straightened his back.

What business did Mr. Dunham have with Wickham?

Darcy intended to find out.

From behind Darcy, a hesitant voice, "Excuse me, sir? Are you well?"

Darcy clenched his fist as Mr. Dunham looked over at him.

"I am well," Darcy said.

"Oh. Excellent." The man stepped in front of Mr. Darcy. He was young with light brown hair and large hands. "My apologies for disturbing you. I had thought you ill. My cousin was quite young when he had an apoplexy, you must understand. I did not mean to cause offense." The young man seemed familiar. Had he not been dancing with Miss Elizabeth?

"Mr. Stewart, is it?"

Mr. Dunham said something to Wickham who nodded and turned towards the opposite end of the hall.

"Yes. You are acquainted with Miss Bennet. I saw—"

"Yes. Yes, I am well. If you will excuse me," Mr. Darcy said, uncaring at his rudeness as Wickham retreated.

"I apologize," Mr. Stewart said again, taking a step back.

"Thank you for your concern," Darcy bowed and turned back to Mr. Dunham who had started walking towards him. Wickham reached the end of the hallway and turned from view.

Mr. Dunham smiled. "Mr. Darcy, I did not see you. Did Miss Bingley send you to check on me?"

"Who was the man you were speaking with?"

"Mr. Wickham?" Mr. Dunham furrowed his brow. "He is assigned to militia records. We were discussing tomorrow's cruise. I wanted to make certain we chose the easiest route."

"Militia records? They have that information?"

"They have excellent maps of the currents. Are you and Mr. Wickham acquainted?"

"From childhood."

"It is a shame he left so quickly. You might have had the chance to reminisce."

A shame. Darcy forced a smile. "Shall we return to the hall? As gentlemen, it is our duty to dance."

"Duty and pleasure," Mr. Dunham said, his shoulders relaxing at Darcy's seeming acceptance of his excuse.

But Darcy knew well enough from his cousin how thin Mr. Dunham's excuse had been. Darcy doubted the paper Wickham had handed Mr. Dunham had anything to do with sea currents.

Whatever their scheme, Darcy intended to find out.

# CHAPTER 11

"What did you say to him?" Elizabeth interrogated her sister.

Lydia laughed. "You two are of a kind, you know this?"

"What did you say?"

"I said he should confess his feelings for you."

Elizabeth's skin went cold. "Feelings?"

"I was jesting. Do not look so alarmed. And then your Mr. Darcy lectured me about my virtue and warned me off Mr. Wickham. I suppose his aunt offered him the same warning she gave you." Lydia cocked her head. "I must say, Mr. Darcy is not as insufferable as he was at Netherfield, though still insufferable enough, I suppose."

"Mr. Darcy is a man with many responsibilities. They take their toll."

"He came to your defense. He said you were so serious because you care for me."

"I do."

Lydia took Elizabeth's hands. "I care for you. But that does not mean I care in any way what the great and venerable Lady Catherine believes of any person. She finds all of us reprehensible! She said as much, you told me."

Elizabeth wished she had the courage to tell Lydia the truth. The words hovered at the tip of her tongue. *It was not Lady Catherine. It was Mr. Darcy.* But Miss Georgiana's secret was not Elizabeth's to share. Certainly not here, in a crowded assembly.

Mrs. Forster called out from the edge of the floor and waved them towards her.

Lydia said, "Whatever does she want?"

It was nothing but conversation.

They ate, drank, and danced a few more sets. Elizabeth moved from one man to the next, but none made her shiver as she had when she rested her fingers atop Mr. Darcy's gloved hands. She called Lydia silly, but there was no greater silliness than developing an infatuation for a man whose proposal one had already refused.

Elizabeth gazed over the hall and told herself she was not hoping to see Mr. Darcy. His serious mien had become, not welcoming, but compelling of her attention.

After the fifth dance, they rested again, taking a glass of punch. Though they had only a light dosing of spirits, the glasses had taken their toll on Elizabeth, making the edges of her vision soft and compelling her to more dramatic movements of her hands and wrists.

Mrs. Forster said, "There is Mr. Stewart with Miss Liverpool, poor woman, so near the shelf at four and twenty!"

Elizabeth mused, "Men remain fresh into their thirties and marriageable beyond, but ladies, like cut flowers, wither and die in seasons."

Mrs. Forster furrowed her brows. "Cut flowers? They die in weeks."

Elizabeth sighed.

Lydia leaned towards Elizabeth, flicking her index finger towards the opposite side of the punch table. "It appears Mr. Bingley is engaged in a flirtation," Lydia said with acid in her voice.

Elizabeth's stomach churned. How was she longing for a glimpse of Mr. Darcy's face when he was the one who had ruined Jane's prospects of Mr. Bingley, who now flirted with other ladies?

But Mr. Bingley was so fickle; perhaps it was best Jane suffer the heartbreak and find another, more faithful, love.

At two and twenty, Jane's bloom was still bright and her stem strong.

Elizabeth shut her eyes.

Lydia said, "I am going to speak with him."

Elizabeth grabbed her sister's wrist. "We cannot —interrupt them twice in the same night."

"Sometimes I wonder if you care for Jane at all."

Elizabeth's anger burned. Her grip tightened.

Lydia said, "You're hurting me!"

Elizabeth threw back the dregs of her glass. "Come then. We shall happen upon them as we fulfill an urgent need for punch."

As they walked towards the punch table, Mr. Bingley looked over and called out, "Miss Elizabeth!"

A touch of Elizabeth's anger cooled at the relief on Mr. Bingley's face, obvious to Elizabeth, who had made an effort in her life to study expressions.

Miss Bingley wrinkled her nose. "Oh yes," she

said. "The Bennet sisters. It seems a fortunate *coincidence* our paths cross and cross again."

Elizabeth smiled. "Most fortunate. Lydia was admiring your fan. The feathers are so very colorful. One would think it too bold a contrast to the delicate pattern of your gown, but Lydia is correct, it suits you."

Mr. Bingley's smile widened. "My sister, since we were children, has always held a remarkable sense of fashion."

Miss Bingley said, eyes narrowing, "I enjoy clothes and have the luxury to afford the highest quality. I've found sometimes other ladies... some few are jealous. It is a blessing you are not one of them."

Elizabeth said, "How could I be? I have never had much regard for clothes beyond their function. My sister has always been the one who studied the fashion plates."

"I have," Lydia agreed. "Lizzy would far rather bury herself in a book and let the entire world fade away as she wanders."

"Miss Whitman," Miss Bingley said, inclining her head towards the Bennet sisters and Miss Forster, allow me to make introductions." As they exchanged names, Elizabeth studied the other young woman. She was handsome with fair hair, though her tresses were neither as thick nor dark as Jane's much lovelier honey locks. Miss Whitman's eyes were blue, and her expression a touch simple as she said, "It is a pleasure to make your acquaintance."

"Likewise," Elizabeth said.

Miss Bingley said, "My brother was about to sign Miss Whitman's dance card."

"Not the seventh, I hope," Lydia cut in.

Mr. Bingley's cheeks flushed. "I am not familiar with that dance," he said stiffly.

Lydia said, "I must write my sister to say you are here and how you asked after her, Mr. Bingley."

"I am certain news will be little more than a triviality to her."

Elizabeth said, "Hardly a triviality. It will delight her."

"How are you acquainted?" Miss Whitman asked. "Mr. Bingley does not have a town accent."

Perhaps Miss Whitman was more perceptive than her vapid expression showed. Elizabeth said, "Mr. Bingley let a home near ours, in Hertfordshire, and we had much opportunity to become acquainted.

"I see," Miss Whitman said.

Miss Bingley said, "We met several people in Hertfordshire. My brother enjoys socializing and makes friends wherever he visits."

"Yes, I remember. One place is much the same as another, he says."

"That is not as I meant it," Mr. Bingley said, his face flushing.

"I had not wished to interrupt," Miss Whitman said. "If this is a private matter."

"Hardly," Though the air was not overly warm, Miss Bingley fluttered her fan. "My brother was just signing your dance card."

"Yes, I was," Mr. Bingley said, amiable again.

"I wonder where Mr. Darcy has gotten off to," Miss Bingley mused. "He was quick to rush off after the first dance."

"Not so surprising," Lydia said. "He is not fond of crowds."

"You have grown so familiar with his preferences after a mere dance?" Miss Bingley said, eyebrows raised.

"Oh, no! It was Lizzy who observed. She is a great observer of character."

Elizabeth dreaded the next words she knew were coming, and they did, "What have you deduced of my character?"

Elizabeth was tempted to give initial impressions: Miss Bingley was a woman obsessed with appearances, most importantly her own. But one glance at Mr. Bingley held Elizabeth's tongue. If Jane was to have any chance of reconciliation, it would not do for Elizabeth to insult Jane's future sister.

At the same time, the possibility of reconciliation was slight. Mr. Darcy may well have already spoken to Mr. Bingley, and if so, Mr. Bingley showed no signs of confessing his heartfelt love for Jane. Perhaps he remembered Jane with some fondness, but that was not the same as love.

How was it the same mother and home had produced two people so different from each other? Mr. Bingley was amiable and Miss Bingley...

Both were exactly what society expected of them.

Elizabeth said, "I believe, you and your brother strive in your lives to achieve all expected of you. And you mostly succeed.

Miss Bingley gave a start.

Mr. Bingley said, "Mostly?"

"No person can achieve another's ideal. If we could, we would not be ourselves at all."

Bingley asked, "And you? I do not—and I say

this with no offense intended—you are not one who struggles to meet anyone's expectations."

"Only my own," Elizabeth said.

"You are selfish then?" Miss Bingley cut in.

"Are we all not selfish, at least in that we truly value? Love. Family. Our homes. The faces we put before the world?"

Mrs. Forster laughed. "A fine jest, Lizzy!" she said, leaning towards the others as though they were sharing some great secret, "Elizabeth always speaks in circles when she jests."

Elizabeth lips twitched. She had not been jesting, but was grateful to Mrs. Forster for easing the tension.

Miss Bingley flipped open her fan and waved it at her chin. "Very amusing," she said with a laugh that did not touch the corners of her eyes. "I suppose we are all selfish in love."

Miss Bingley fluttered the fan again, and Elizabeth's neck and shoulders relaxed.

Miss Bingley was afraid. It was a truth Elizabeth had not understood. Mr. Bingley's father had made their fortune in trade, which Mr. Bingley had inherited, but Miss Bingley had no means to maintain or improve her situation outside of gaining a husband. She and Elizabeth were not so different, except for

Elizabeth and her sisters' relative poverty. Perhaps their country upbringing had been a blessing. Miss Bingley's fortune only did so much to mitigate her bloodlines, and unlike Elizabeth, she would have faced this truth from a young age.

"There they are. Darcy!" Bingley said, waving across the room to Mr. Darcy and Mr. Dunham who stood by an entrance, looking over the room. Darcy nodded, and they started across the hall.

Mr. Dunham was speaking, and Mr. Darcy nodded, his hands clasped behind his back. He moved stiffly, back straight, chin tucked, while Mr. Dunham spoke with animation, smiling, fingers punctuating a point.

Mr. Dunham's gaze fixed on Miss Bingley, and his smile widened. He walked to her, took her hand and brushed a kiss against her glove. "I am sorry I kept you waiting for such a long time. I was fortunate enough to cross paths with a mutual friend—"

"Acquaintance," Mr. Darcy said.

"Yes...acquaintance then, who assured us that the route for tomorrow's excursion promises to be both clear and safe."

"Will you be walking and having a picnic?" Lydia asked. "My sister is so very fond of walking."

Mr. Dunham laughed. "No. I have invited Mr.

Bingley and his sister for a pleasure cruise on my boat. You should come as well, Miss Lydia. And Miss Elizabeth and Miss Forster, of course. We shall leave in the afternoon and have dinner on the sea."

Lydia clapped her hands together. "How wonderful!"

"We do not wish to impose," Elizabeth said.

Lydia glared at her, but Mr. Dunham said, "It is no imposition. There is room enough for a few more souls. Have you ever taken a jaunt by sea?"

Lydia shook her head. "Never. And I shall treasure the memory every day I draw breath. Lizzy, we must go. It would be impolite not to."

Reluctantly, Elizabeth nodded. "Provided Mrs. Forster has no objections, as she is our chaperone."

Mrs. Forster gave them both a bright smile. "We cannot thank you enough, Mr. Dunham."

Mr. Dunham waved a hand. "You needn't thank me at all. A friend of Mr. Bingley is a friend of mine. Give me the address of your residence, and I will forward all you need to know. We shall leave at half three. And return after dinner."

The next dance was called, and Elizabeth glanced at her card. One benefit to having waylaid Mr. Bingley was Mr. Wickham would fear to solicit

Elizabeth or Lydia for their dance in Mr. Darcy's presence.

Which meant all Elizabeth had to accomplish was remaining in Mr. Darcy's presence until the seventh dance was complete.

Mr. Stewart approached the group. He stood outside their circle and in a quiet voice said, "Excuse me, Miss Lydia."

Lydia turned to him. "Mr. Stewart?"

"Our dance," he said, bowing.

"Yes," Lydia said, looking down at her dance card.

"Go on," Mrs. Forster said. "Lizzy, did you not have a dance with Mr. Wickham?"

"How odd of him to leave without a word," Mr. Dunham said. "Perhaps he had some sudden duties?"

"Perhaps," Elizabeth agreed. Hopefully, he had fled the assembly, not to return for the evening.

"As a friend of Mr. Bingley, I cannot in good conscience permit you to miss your dance, Miss Elizabeth," Mr. Dunham said with a bow. He held out his hand. "If I may."

"I..." Elizabeth's stomach sank. She could not

refuse him without insult, but accepting would antagonize Miss Bingley who already held Elizabeth in poor regard.

"Miss Elizabeth looks pale," Miss Bingley said. "We would not wish to tax her constitution."

"Nonsense," Mrs. Hurst said. "You are not ill, are you? None has as robust a constitution as Miss Elizabeth. A mere dance will not tax her. Go on, Miss Elizabeth."

Elizabeth forced a smile and accepted.

Elizabeth and Mr. Dunham took their places, side-by-side, hands raised, hers resting atop his. Six dancers away, Lydia stood with Mr. Stewart, who said something to make Lydia smile.

The music began.

They stepped apart, turned, and met again, face-to-face. Mr. Dunham was handsome, fair-haired with a strong jaw, wide shoulders and a frame only slightly gone to fat. His fine, bespoke tailoring hid his gut, but as the dance continued, Elizabeth noted a sheen of sweat on his brow at his exertion.

In his defense, this was a quicker, country dance. The type Elizabeth usually enjoyed. She danced away, turned and clapped, her dress swirling at her feet. They met again, and the music slowed.

"You are, as Mrs. Hurst said, in robust health."

Elizabeth laughed.

As they circled each other, Elizabeth noted Mr. Darcy standing at the edge of the floor, watching.

Mr. Darcy was adept at staring. Elizabeth remembered this well from her time at Rosings Park. Not that she suspected, this time, he was contemplating another proposal.

"What is it, Miss Bennet?"

Elizabeth turned her gaze back to Mr. Dunham's eyes and said, "Nothing."

They opened their right hands and stepped away from each other, side by side. Elizabeth wiped her sleeve over her brow.

They came back together.

Mr. Dunham said, "I do not suppose Mr. Darcy told you we attended school together, as boys."

Elizabeth smiled. "Was he as serious then as he is now?"

"Oh yes. Though in his defense, Darcy was older than I and one of the head boys."

"Mr. Darcy is the sort who courts responsibility."

"Is this your measure of his character?"

Elizabeth shook her head. "It takes no measure

of character to recognize the obvious, Mr. Dunham."

They stepped away again, wove around three others in the path of a braid. Lydia gave Elizabeth a nod as she passed. Elizabeth danced with a second partner, lifting her skirt and turning to a young, chubby officer who moved with grace and lightness on his feet. They exchanged names and pleasantries before the dance returned them each to their original partners.

Elizabeth said, "I suppose you and Mr. Darcy lost touch in the intervening years?"

"Yes, to my shame. I fear, despite my best efforts, I have not made as good an impression on him as I would wish."

Elizabeth could sympathize, but she did not wish to reveal her own thoughts to Mr. Dunham. He was too charming, and Elizabeth had made such a mistake already in trusting Mr. Wickham. Not that Mr. Darcy's judgment was always correct. "Who was the man you met with whom Mr. Darcy insists is an acquaintance and not a friend?" Elizabeth suspected, but she wanted to hear it from Mr. Dunham's lips.

"Mr. Wickham. He works in records. I wanted to be certain there would be no obstacles to our jaunt tomorrow. I did not know of his acquaintance with Mr. Darcy until this evening. It seems there is some...animosity."

That much was obvious, and Elizabeth nodded.

"You would not happen to know what set the two men at odds?" Mr. Dunham asked. "Neither Mr. Wickham nor Mr. Darcy spoke of their history."

Mr. Wickham was charming, and if the meeting between the two of them was innocuous, Mr. Dunham deserved a warning lest he seek a deeper relationship with the scoundrel. But Elizabeth could not share all Mr. Darcy had revealed to her. Elizabeth said, "I fear Mr. Wickham has a reputation for being fond of cards. Perhaps overly fond. I should not offer him a loan, if I were you.

"Oh, I see. Mr. Darcy was unfortunate enough to make such a loan then?"

Elizabeth shrugged. "I cannot say I understand all that has happened between Mr. Darcy and Mr. Wickham. Mr. Darcy and I are not close."

"I thank you for your warning. I will not engage in any games of chance with Mr. Wickham, and any business between us, I shall keep between us so as not to trouble Mr. Darcy or Mr. Bingley, who may himself have made a similar error."

They danced away again in the opposite direction as before, weaving and spinning. While Elizabeth maintained her mask of politeness, Mr. Dunham's words disturbed her. What further business would Mr. Wickham and Mr. Dunham rightfully have? Further, while Elizabeth could claim no knowledge of the inner workings with the militia, was it not the Navy's role to handle information like sea currents? Perhaps the militia and navy kept their records in the same building?

If so, then Mr. Dunham still would have done better to approach a naval officer rather than Mr. Wickham. The story rang false. Or perhaps it was how Mr. Dunham's gaze abstracted as he told it.

When they came back together again, Elizabeth asked, "And how did you become acquainted with Miss Bingley?"

Mr. Dunham remarked upon meeting Miss Bingley at an assembly and crossing paths with her again at a mutual acquaintance's dinner. "Miss Bingley is a marvel, is she not? She has had some troubles, because of her father making his income in trade. We of the Ton concern ourselves too much with bloodlines. The world is changing. Have you seen the new French looms, which weave faster and with greater meticulousness than our traditional methods?"

"I should think it improper to speak of grand French inventions, considering our current conflict."

"A conflict we will win, looms aside. I merely say the world is changing. Look at the Americas. Men are making vast fortunes in those untamed lands."

Elizabeth said, "I doubt Miss Bingley has much desire to find her future in untamed lands."

Mr. Dunham smiled. "And neither do I. I point out things are not as they were, and in another hundred years, who knows what marvels humanity may have achieved. Will titles or the age of our wealth matter in such times?"

They stepped away and returned, performing the final movements of the dance. Elizabeth's gaze passed over the dancers. Where was Lydia? Mr. Stewart had also exited the floor, it seemed.

The music ended.

"Thank you for a most interesting dance." Mr. Dunham said with a bow.

Elizabeth curtsied. Being deemed interesting was hardly flattery, not that Elizabeth minded. She said, "Yes, most invigorating."

Where was Lydia?

"Miss Elizabeth!" Miss Bingley walked towards them, a young officer at her side. "Mr. Dunham, I trust you both enjoyed your dance."

Mr. Dunham bowed to Miss Bingley and said, "Greatly, and greatly I look forward to ours."

Mr. Stewart stood by the Ratafia table with another officer. Mrs. Forster at the opposite side, near the room's corner, chatting with Mrs. Hurst. Elizabeth smothered a sigh. If it was anyone but her sister, Elizabeth would wait. But Lydia was a magnet for trouble. Elizabeth should at least attempt to find the girl.

"Miss Bingley, by chance, have you seen my sister?"

"Miss Lydia and the young officer? I suppose they returned to your friend."

Except she was not with Mrs. Forster. Elizabeth curtsied again. "Yes, of course."

Miss Bingley's eyes narrowed. "You do not believe she has gotten into any mischief, do you?"

"No. I am merely winded," Elizabeth said.

"You, winded? I cannot imagine."

Mr. Dunham said, "It was a challenging dance."

"For those less inclined to physical activity than Miss Elizabeth, I suppose."

Mr. Dunham either did not hear or ignored the

venom in Miss Bingley's tone. "Come now, Miss Elizabeth is devoted to her sister, which can only be to her approbation."

"Yes, I have noted Miss Elizabeth Bennet is very devoted to family. With so many sisters, it is to be expected."

"So many?" Mr. Dunham asked.

Miss Bingley pursed her lips, but Mr. Dunham had turned his gaze to Elizabeth.

Miss Bingley was a dratted fool! If she could be quiet long enough for Elizabeth to excuse herself, Miss Bingley would have Mr. Dunham again to herself. Elizabeth certainly did not wish to court with him.

"Lydia must have stepped out for some air," Elizabeth said, waving towards the entrance. "I shall speak with Mrs. Forster. Excuse me."

The others agreed. As Elizabeth stepped away from the group, she turned and found herself near stumbling into Mr. Darcy's arms.

# CHAPTER 12

It was rude to stare and ruder to glare, but Mr. Darcy did both as he watched Mr. Dunham lead Miss Elizabeth to the dance floor. As they spoke, Elizabeth's expression moved through consideration and laughter to rest on amiability belied by the focus of her gaze.

What was their topic of conversation?

Was he flirting with Miss Elizabeth?

Darcy fantasized a moment of taking Mr. Dunham outside and engaging in fisticuffs, to defend Miss Bingley's honor, of course. He had no further interest in Miss Elizabeth.

Miss Elizabeth smiled again, and Darcy's hands clenched.

Darcy would do better to determine where Mr.

Wickham had run off to. With his father passed, Darcy had no reason to pretend conciliation with the man. Darcy tore his eyes away from the dancers and let his gaze pass over the rest of the room.

Mr. Wickham was not in the room.

The worst of it was, beyond the suspicious exchange of words between the two men, Darcy had no reason to dislike Mr. Dunham. He and Miss Elizabeth's hands clasped again, and once more she smiled.

Little reason then.

When the dance ended, Darcy, though it strained propriety, approached the couple. He was not alone. Miss Bingley crossed from the opposite side. Miss Elizabeth curtsied, turned and stumbled. Darcy reached out, steadying her.

Miss Elizabeth smelled of lavender. She gave a nervous laugh. "I did not see you."

"I had not expected you to turn."

"Have you seen my sister?"

"I believe Mrs. Forster was dancing with her husband, but as to your sister," Darcy pressed his lips together, as he thought. "She was dancing, and I suppose she went with the young man for punch."

But Mr. Darcy had not seen them. Mr. Darcy had not given a whit of his attention to Miss Lydia, and would not have noticed unless the young lady addressed him, his gaze his gaze being so fixed upon Miss Elizabeth. Darcy looked out over the group. He spotted Mrs. Forster and Miss Hurst, caught in what seemed like an animated discussion. Miss Lydia was missing.

Darcy said, "I am certain she is well. This is an assembly."

"Yes, of course." Elizabeth shrugged, displacing his hands and gave him a curtsy. "I apologize again."

"Take my arm. I will walk you to Mrs. Forster."

Darcy extended his arm, and to his surprise, Elizabeth took it without protest. They walked together.

Mr. Darcy asked, "It seems you and Mr. Dunham had a pleasant dance. He is one for conversation."

"Much of it about you."

"You did not find him amiable?"

"I found him amiable and inquisitive." The emphasis on 'inquisitive' and the irritation in her tone gratified Darcy.

Darcy asked, "Inquisitive?"

"He wished to know the history between you and Mr. Wickham. I said nothing directly but intimated Mr. Wickham had a fondness for cards and a propensity not to pay back the monies he owed."

Darcy's lips quirked. "You are clever."

"I told him the truth, if not all of it."

"And how would you judge his character?" Darcy had meant it at first as a quip, but he found himself interested in Miss Elizabeth's perspective. She had misjudged Wickham and himself, though Darcy recognized his own culpability in the latter at least. He had misjudged her upon first impression too, declaring her tolerable, and worse, she had overheard his judgment. Darcy could not blame her for her initial disapprobation.

Miss Elizabeth said, "He is amiable, charming and nervous. But my judgment is often flawed."

"As is mine," Darcy admitted.

"There she is," Elizabeth said, waving a hand towards Mrs. Forster.

"Ours is the next dance."

"It is, yes."

"You are worried."

Elizabeth forced a laugh. "Lydia is likely getting air, and that is all. She takes great joy in troubling me."

Mrs. Hurst's eyes widened as Darcy and Elizabeth approached.

Elizabeth asked, "Have you seen Lydia?"

"I had thought her dancing with Mr. Stewart." She cocked her head and said, "Perhaps she had a sudden need—female business, you understand."

Elizabeth understood, and she also knew it was not her sister's time. Though she could have needed to relieve herself of the plenitude of the punch.

Mrs. Forster said, "She will be along, soon enough."

As Lydia's chaperone, Mrs. Forster should have concerned herself more about Lydia's whereabouts.

An ache started in Elizabeth's temples. She said, "Perhaps she felt the need for some fresh air. I will find her."

Do not take too long, Lizzy. They will call the sixth dance soon."

The dance Mr. Darcy had chosen.

"I will accompany you," Mr. Darcy said.

It was one thing for Mr. Darcy to walk with her unchaperoned in the middle of a crowded assembly, quite another for Mr. Darcy to walk her outside of the hall on his own. In either case, venturing outside without a chaperone risked Elizabeth's virtue. Though such things happened, and this was not London. Brighton was reputed for laxness in such proprieties.

Mrs. Forster turned to Mrs. Hurst. "If you'll excuse me," she said. "I will help Lizzy find her dear sister. If she comes to you, tell her we are looking for her."

Mrs. Hurst nodded. "Of course. I will keep watch on Caroline, as my brother seems occupied with Miss Whitman."

Elizabeth glanced across the floor to where Mr. Bingley and Miss Whitman stood with another group of ladies and gentlemen, all conversing. Was Mr. Bingley enamored of Miss Whitman? With his back partially turned to her and Miss Whitman too far away to gauge her expression, Elizabeth had no way to guess.

Elizabeth would have preferred to leave both Mrs. Forster in Mr. Darcy behind, but at least Mr. Darcy would support Elizabeth should Lydia have found herself in an unsavory situation.

Elizabeth's worst fear was that Lydia had somehow stumbled across Mr. Wickham and now was engaged in flirtation. Lydia had ignored Elizabeth's warning, and Elizabeth could not know what her sister would do.

They left the room, walked down the hall to the privies.

Elizabeth stepped inside, nose wrinkling at the

smell of waste, and called out for her sister. Lydia did not respond, and after a few moments, Elizabeth left.

"I wonder where she got off to then," Mrs. Forster asked. "It is warm in the assembly hall. Perhaps she stepped outside."

"On her own?" Mr. Darcy asked.

Elizabeth smiled at Mr. Darcy's incredulous tone. Lydia had been running off on her own since they had arrived. The gambling hell. The time she had joined the jugglers and dancers on the Promenade. The swimming off on her own and their rescue of Ernest the seal.

Elizabeth said, "Let us check."

They stepped outside, and a cool, salt-scented breeze whipped over them. Elizabeth's curls tickled her temples and forehead.

A line of carriages angled out from the curbside. A lantern sat on either side of the door, hung from stone posts. Beyond, the three-quarter moon shone, giving the stonework along the pavements a silvery sheen.

Elizabeth's stomach churned. At first, she had just assumed Lydia had gotten herself into some trouble, but not the sort that would have her disappear.

"Lydia?" Elizabeth called out. She walked downstairs and swept her gaze along the street.

Mrs. Forster said, "Lydia must be inside somewhere, dancing. The next dance will start soon. You needn't worry."

Elizabeth sighed. Perhaps Mrs. Forster was right. But just as Elizabeth turned back to the assembly hall, someone giggled. The sound came from Elizabeth's left, and as she dashed, she heard it again in the space between the assembly and a neighboring building.

"Lydia?" Elizabeth berated herself. Her sister was a magnet for trouble, and Elizabeth was here to keep her from the worst of it. A task she continually failed. If Lydia was injured, Elizabeth would blame herself. If she had gotten herself into different trouble, Elizabeth would blame both of them.

The rustle of fabric, the scrape of shoe leather against stone.

"Lydia? What are you doing?" Elizabeth walked down the narrow space between the assembly hall and the neighboring building. "Come out, now."

"Shh!" Lydia squatted on the ground, her dress sweeping a circle around her. "Stay back."

Elizabeth froze. "What is it?"

"A cat," Lydia explained. "I thought I heard a cat."

Mr. Darcy and Mrs. Forster came up behind Elizabeth. Darcy asked, "What is it?"

"Lydia heard a cat."

Mrs. Forster said, "Oh dear! Was it a kitten? When I was 12, we found an entire litter of kittens at the base of the folly, a quarter mile from the main house. Oh, the poor pitiful things! They were puffs of mewing fur, so sweet. Their ears were still folded over, just slightly, and their eyes were the brightest blue." Mrs. Forster tried to push past Lydia, who held out her arm as she stood. "No, it is gone."

"When? I saw nothing move."

"He was black with a patch of white on his belly, I think." Lydia explained, giving a near-perfect description of Sammy, one of Longbourn's barn cats.

Elizabeth, now suspicious, squinted down the alleyway. Five feet further along was a dark alcove, but without walking closer, Elizabeth could not see who or what was inside.

Lydia said, "Come, the dancing will begin again shortly. I do not think the cat is coming back."

If Mr. Darcy had not been with them, Elizabeth

would have continued to the alcove and seen for herself. But Lydia took a firm grip on Mrs. Forster's arm, and Elizabeth, not wishing to put her sister's reputation in danger if she had been flirting or, heaven forbid, doing something more with—!

Elizabeth could not bear to think of it further.

Mr. Darcy said, "A cat, was it?"

Mrs. Forster said, "Lydia and Elizabeth both are very fond of animals. Why, they rescued a seal just yesterday."

"A seal? From the sea? Did it wash ashore?"

"In a manner of speaking." Lydia said, "Ernest was in great distress. If Elizabeth had not worn that ridiculous bathing gown, I do not know how we would've kept it still long enough to extricate his back fins from the net."

Mr. Darcy shook his head.

"We should return to the assembly," Miss Forster said. "My husband has promised to dance with me the new dance, and I shall enjoy it, I have resolved."

"I suppose I shall enjoy watching it," Lydia said. "As my dance partner is absent."

"He may return," Mrs. Forster said. "He seemed enamored of you."

"Merely polite," Elizabeth said.

When they returned to the assembly, dancers gathered at the center of the ballroom.

The musicians began to play. Mr. Darcy said, "Come. Our dance."

Elizabeth leaned closer to him and whispered, "You did not wish…if you do not wish to dance, I will not insist."

"Do you wish dance?"

Elizabeth nodded. She was tired of chasing her sister and tired of running away from whatever emotion was developing inside of her for Mr. Darcy. He would not propose again. And Elizabeth did not wish him to. But she would enjoy this dance. And when it was over, she would put dancing with him from her mind.

They took their places with the other dancers and clasped their hands and spun away from each other. Mr. Darcy guided Elizabeth, and they danced, stepping and spinning as the movements brought them together and apart again.

## CHAPTER 13

Darcy's dance with Elizabeth went far too swiftly. She was oddly quiet, her gaze abstracted. Perhaps she still despised him as she had stated at the culmination of his failed proposal. But she had not despised him earlier. Her quick mind and wit had been on full display, dark eyes glittering as she discussed her impressions of Mr. Dunham.

No, the distraction had come after: Her sister. The alley. The cat.

Darcy had thought Georgiana a handful when she was younger, but from this brief interaction, Darcy recognized Lydia as more troublesome.

Not to say mean-hearted, but troublesome.

Darcy asked, "Does your sister often chase cats?"

Elizabeth's right eye twitched, but she maintained an amiable smile as she said, "My sister is a caring soul, if sometimes reckless."

Elizabeth's anger was plain in the lowering of her voice at the word "reckless," and Darcy realized he had neither seen nor heard a cat. If Lydia had stepped outside for another reason than air, to meet with someone unsavory, perhaps, it would explain the tension in Miss Elizabeth's hands and shoulders as she moved, with grace if not enthusiasm, through the complex steps of the dance.

This dance at least did not have them switching partners, though they came apart and together often.

If what Darcy suspected Elizabeth suspected was true, then Lydia risked not only her reputation but that of her family. Lydia risked not only her prospects but those of her sisters. For all the faults Darcy had outlined in regard to Elizabeth's family, a lack of love had not been among them.

Darcy said, "Your sister Lydia may be spirited, but I doubt she would risk more than she ought— for a cat."

Elizabeth's eyes widened and she met his gaze

for the first time since they had started the dance. She took in a breath through parted lips and breathed out her nose. "If you were a solicitous gentlemen, and I a lady expecting of such gestures, I would thank you for this offer of comfort."

A thread tightened in Darcy's stomach, and he wished to slip his arm around her back, rest his hand on her hip and pull her close in the way of a scandal. The seventh dance. But Darcy asked, and Elizabeth agreed, it would imply something he could not offer again. He squeezed her fingers and held back the need to kiss her.

"Whatever has happened, I will help you. You need only ask."

Elizabeth ran her tongue between her lips. They stepped back, one-two-three, turned, and clapped.

The dance ended.

"Thank you," Elizabeth said.

"Always." Darcy bowed. The dance was over, and he could not stand to watch the next one, knowing he would never hold Elizabeth in his arms.

Blast his heart! It was as reckless as a young girl chasing invisible cats.

Miss Lydia called out to Elizabeth as she curtsied. "If you'll excuse me," Darcy said, at the same point Miss Elizabeth said, "If I may."

Both were silent, and Darcy, knew that if he did not step away, he would ask her for the second dance and to the devil with the consequences.

"I must go," Elizabeth said, gesturing to her sister.

"Yes."

Darcy was the first to turn. Bingley fell into step with Darcy as he climbed the stairs from the hall.

"What did Miss Elizabeth say to send you off as if the devil himself dogged your heels?"

"Nothing. She said nothing."

"Something has upset you, Darcy. You cover your emotions with coldness, but when that fails, your face is an open book."

"Walk with me," Darcy ordered.

Bingley, ever the excellent friend followed. They left the assembly and stood out on the cobbled street running before it. Darcy closed his eyes, letting the cool sea air ease his ardor.

"Did she speak you of Miss Jane?" Bingley sighed. "I suppose her sister has found another love."

"Miss Elizabeth did not say."

"Would she?"

Shame squeezed Darcy's chest, making it difficult to breathe. As a friend, he should confess his proposal to Elizabeth and her revelation of Miss Jane Bennet's feelings. Bingley had given him the opportunity. It would absolve Darcy's conscience. But Bingley's temper, while slow to ignite, burned hot. He would, rightfully, distrust any further advice Darcy offered. And then Bingley and his sister would be swept up in Mr. Dunham and Wickham's scheme, whatever it was.

No, Darcy could not afford to confess. Not yet.

Instead, he waved Bingley towards the alley. "This way," Darcy said guiding his friend to the alley. If Miss Lydia had engaged in an assignation with something other than a cat, the young man would have fled as soon as Darcy, Elizabeth and the others had left. But if nothing else, the narrow space offered privacy. It was dim and narrow, with only a hint of the above moonlight filtering between the two tall buildings. The ground was damp and smelled of fish.

"Darcy, why the devil are we here? It stinks of rotting fish."

An alcove, wide enough for two people standing close, led to a second door to the building. Darcy tried the knob, but it was locked. He walked until he saw a second. He reached the end of the alley and turned the corner to a small garden. From a large, open door, Darcy heard the faint call of violins and a flute.

Bingley caught up, his footfalls dulled by the damp stone. "You are looking for someone. Who?"

Darcy shrugged. "Earlier, Miss Elizabeth and Mrs. Forster found Miss Lydia out here. She said she had heard a cat, but..."

"You believe she—?"

"No!" Darcy would not impugn Miss Elizabeth's honor by making suppositions about her sister. Not out loud at least.

"Then why are we here?"

"I needed assurance we are alone. Wickham and Mr. Dunham are working together on something." Darcy whispered, explaining what he had overseen and Mr. Dunham's explanation.

"It is thin, Darcy. Perhaps Mr. Dunham is fond of cards."

Darcy had not told Bingley the whole of Wickham's betrayal. Bingley knew of the gambling and the money Darcy had lent him, but he did not know about Wickham's seduction of Georgiana. Only Darcy, his cousin, and Miss Elizabeth were privy to that information. Darcy said, "Wickham's character is worse than you know. It is possible Mr. Dunham is, as you said, fond of gambling. But if they are more than acquaintances, it puts your sister in a precarious position. She is making no secret of her interest in Mr. Dunham and he is effusive in his courtship. Your sister Mrs. Hurst also expressed concerns that Mr. Dunham's father has made some poor investments, and fear of loss can make men do desperate things.

"Men *and* women," Bingley said with a nod. "Darcy, you are my dearest friend, and I could never doubt either your judgment or your honor. If you believe Mr. Dunham poses a danger to my sister, then I will tell her to call it off."

"No!" Darcy did not want to ruin another Bingley's chance at happiness. Not on such thin evidence. He had made that mistake once, and it cost him his chance with Miss Elizabeth Bennet. Darcy said, "I do not know for certain, and your sister will despise you to her dying breath if you stand between her and her happiness."

Bingley sighed. "If she even listened to me. Caroline has always done as she likes."

"I have already written to my solicitor to look into Mr. Dunham's finances. But we are far from town, and inquiries take time. Better we learned what we can here."

Bingley nodded. "I suppose this means I must

subject myself to that cursed cruise. It will appease Caroline at least. Though I warn you, as I warned her, I may puke."

"If you could direct your spewing to an available bucket, or better, over the side of the ship, we shall find it more agreeable."

Bingley laughed. He clapped Darcy on the shoulder." I am glad to know you are not also falling into an infatuation with a Bennet. That way lies heartbreak, my friend."

"I know," Darcy said with a nod. But even as he returned to the assembly, Miss Elizabeth and Miss Lydia stood together at the edge of the floor as, in pairs, dancers moved close enough to feel the heat of their partners as they stepped and turned.

Miss Elizabeth glanced up as Darcy and Bingley crossed the entrance. Darcy averted his gaze. If only he could turn away from his own feelings so easily.

# CHAPTER 14

Elizabeth waited until she and Lydia were under the duvet in their shared bed to ask about the cat.

"It was a black cat with a touch of white on his belly."

"Odd how Sammy ranged so far and found his way back to us here in Brighton."

Lydia yanked the duvet up to her chin. "You are the worst sister. I may not be as clever as the accomplished Lizzy Bennet, but I know it is possible for there to exist more than one mostly black cat in the world."

Maybe Lydia was right. Maybe Elizabeth was being unreasonable. Except if there had been a cat, as with Ernest the seal, Lydia would have insisted

Elizabeth and the rest of them search. No, Lydia was covering up her true intentions. And Elizabeth suspected her true intentions posed a grave danger to the young woman's virtue.

"It seems Mr. Darcy has grown fond of you, Lizzy." What happened when you visited Charlotte? Did you and Mr. Darcy engage in an assignation?"

No!"

"And yet, you accuse me of improper meetings in alleys with cats. You must understand how insufferable you are sometimes," Lydia said.

Elizabeth leaned back on her pillow. It was too soft, and as she sank into its depths, the pillow molded about her head. Muffling her hearing.

Elizabeth said, "Lydia, I hope you understand it is my love for you, as your sister, that makes me ask such questions."

"And my actions reflect on all of us. I know," Lydia muttered.

Elizabeth rolled over towards Lydia, sat up on her elbow, and pounded the pillow. Before folding it in half and laying back down upon it. It was a marginal improvement.

The worst of it was, Elizabeth *had* become insufferable. She was no model of virtue, her thoughts straying most improperly to how Mr.

Darcy's lips would feel on her own, how she would press her body against his, the strength of him, his tension easing under her fingers and becoming a different excitement.

No, Elizabeth was not as virtuous as she wished. She knew the power of a man's lips on hers and the feel of his embrace. Worse, to be fantasizing of such things about Mr. Darcy now, without even the possibility of marriage. A possibility she had done away with in rejecting his proposal.

Had Mr. Darcy proposed without offering any warning? He had stared at Elizabeth. He had interrupted her walks with awkward conversation. Perhaps that was his method of courtship? And then he had proposed through a string of insults. He had betrayed Jane.

Elizabeth was worse than unvirtuous; she was also disloyal.

But Mr. Darcy was not entirely dreadful. He had risked both his reputation and his sister's in trusting Elizabeth with his secrets. Now, with Mr. Wickham here, Elizabeth could warn her sister off of him. Not that Lydia had believed Elizabeth.

Lydia found Elizabeth insufferable, and Elizabeth had done little to prove herself different. But if she could not share Mr. Darcy secrets, she could share one of her own."

Elizabeth's stomach churned and her cheeks burned with mortification as said, "I am not so pure as you might imagine. I met a gentleman at an assembly, and we…"

Lydia asked, "Did what?" She flipped over and tugged on Elizabeth's sleeve. "Did he kiss you?"

"Yes." Elizabeth remembered the flutter in her stomach at John Marley pressing his lips against hers, and then his tongue, sweeping awkwardly at the seam of her lips. Elizabeth, struck by the oddness of the sensation, had frozen, and John, a local tenant's son whom Elizabeth had met and danced with at three assemblies, had pulled back, punch-scented breath tickling beneath her nose, and asked, "Are you well?" He'd run his hand through his thick, light brown hair.

Elizabeth, heart pounding, had said, "I felt faint, that is all."

John's face broke into a grin. "Yes, I too. But you liked it?"

Elizabeth had liked some of it, the power of his arms holding her, the heat of him, and how she wanted for something she did not define, but it also confused her. Threaded through this desire was a fear she would lose herself.

"Yes. Nothing else. During an assembly. We stole away."

"Who was it?"

"A tenant's son."

"You minx! Has he married or is he pining for you?"

Pining? Elizabeth smiled. "No, he is married."

"And you were not jealous?"

"Hardly. It was a moment of weakness."

"Yes, a tenant's son would have been a disastrous match. I cannot imagine what Papa would have said."

Elizabeth could imagine, though she had not thought of it until after she'd returned, alone, to the assembly. Elizabeth had been more concerned with John's smile, and the way her thoughts had spun in circles thinking of him.

"Was it nice?" Lydia asked.

Elizabeth nodded. "Nice and scary and strange and…"

"Have you kissed anyone since?"

"No."

"Why ever not?"

"I wish to marry for love, and if I ruin myself

on an infatuation, I will never know a loving match."

"But is not infatuation a part of love? Mama always speaks fondly of her courtship with Papa."

"And are they happy with each other now?"

"It is only because Papa hides his true self behind jests. And I suppose Mama feels she failed, as we have no brothers."

Lydia's observation shocked Elizabeth. She had always thought Lydia silly, but no person was wholly one thing or another. Elizabeth said, "I do not mean to be insufferable. I just worry."

"I too wish to find love," Lydia murmured. "But how will we know what our heart says if we do not listen to it?"

"I do not know," Elizabeth said.

What was the difference between love and desire? How did one judge one's heart when it was pulled into different directions? Elizabeth could not forgive Mr. Darcy for the harm he had caused Jane, and neither could she deny her growing interest in him. It would be easiest to walk away, as she had that night with John. Easiest and wisest, and yet, tomorrow, she would join him and Mr. Bingley on this foolish cruise.

"I do not believe I will run away," Lydia said. "If offered a kiss, I would take a second."

Elizabeth realized she had erred. Lydia's voice was wistful and curious. She had not, as yet, compromised her virtue. And Elizabeth, in revealing her own missteps, had expanded in Lydia's mind the scope of her own mistakes.

"Please, take care," Elizabeth said.

Lydia laughed. "You goose! I will share your secret with no one, not even Mr. Darcy, who seems, in his own way, fond of you."

"What makes you think he is fond?" Elizabeth asked.

"He stares so. And he defends you. If Mr. Darcy had not been so plain in his assertion that you were merely tolerable, Lizzy, I would think he held some affection. Are you certain nothing happened at Rosings to change his heart?"

"If his heart changed, it hardened against me," Elizabeth said, honestly if not with complete truth. "I am tired." She punctuated her statement with a forced yawn.

Lydia said, "Yes, we have much to do tomorrow to turn Mr. Bingley's heart back to our sister. Mr. Darcy can wait."

# CHAPTER 15

Bingley's skin took on a greenish cast as they stepped onto the deck.

Besides the Bingley's, Mrs. Hurst, Miss Elizabeth, her sister, and Mrs. Forster, and Darcy himself, there were two other men. The first was a white-whiskered older gentleman named Mr. Stanton who wore a lightweight coat and linen shirt, no cravat, breeches and well-worn leather boots. He smelled of tobacco and periodically reached into his jacket to finger a pipe, sometimes placing it between his teeth but not lighting it.

The second was a young man, Mr. Whitmore. Mr. Stanton introduced Mr. Whitmore as his nephew. They did not show much family resemblance. Mr. Whitmore was thin with mouse brown hair and a quiet, measuring gaze that made the back of Mr. Darcy's neck itch. Both had been on the ship when Mr. Darcy, Mr. Bingley, Mrs. Hurst and Miss Bingley arrived.

To Mr. Darcy's surprise, after loading picnic supplies for the ship and storing them below, the servants left. Mr. Dunham explained, "It is not a large boat, and with Whitmore's help, we can easily manage a short jaunt along the shoreline."

"How are you and Mr. Whitmore acquainted?" Mr. Darcy asked. Mr. Whitmore did not wear the reds of the militiaman, and the slight slouch of his posture in combination with the rough, country edge of his accent made it clear, despite his clothing, he was not an ordinary gentleman.

Mr. Dunham smiled. "We share a passion for boating, but Mr. Whitmore's boat is under repair."

Mr. Darcy and Mr. Whitmore exchanged greetings, but with neither being much inclined towards small talk, Darcy excused himself to help Miss Bingley and her brother settle themselves on the ship.

The Bennets and Mrs. Forster arrived next.

Lydia, upon boarding, dashed to the ship's prow and back again, observing the shape of the hull, the glossiness of the ship's decks, and the intricacies of the knotted sails with joyous, if incoherent observations.

Darcy clapped his friend on the shoulder. "Focus on the horizon," he advised.

"Does it help?"

"Richard says so. He had to travel by sea to the continent."

Bingley nodded, taking a few steps to the dead center of the widest part of the deck and seating himself upon one of the cushions placed there for that purpose.

The ship's rocking increased as they pulled out of the harbor. Above, sails swelled, and they picked up speed.

"Lizzy! Look, I think it is Ernest!" Lydia pointed over the side of the deck, leaning forward, carelessly holding on as she waved down at the hull of the ship with her free hand.

"Lydia!" Elizabeth pulled on her sister's arm.

Lydia wrenched it free. "I am fine, Lizzy. Don't you wish to see?" She pointed.

Elizabeth, showing more caution than her sister, walked to the edge of the deck and looked over.

Five seals swam alongside the boat. They were too far away for Elizabeth to make out any specifics of their forms as they leapt and submerged through the waves like a thread through fabric. Elizabeth said, I cannot tell one from the next."

"Ernest is smaller, and he has the scar."

"Who is Ernest?" Mr. Darcy asked.

"We rescued him," Lydia explained. "While we were bathing. I swam out to a sandbar and saw him. Lizzy was wearing her foolish bathing dress, but it came in useful to hold him down so we could get the netting off of his back flippers."

"Ah, yes. I remember the tale from last evening." The boat rocked over a wave, and Mr. Darcy grabbed Elizabeth's arm. "Careful."

Elizabeth took hold of the deck rail with both hands. "Thank you," she said.

Mr. Stanton let out a belly laugh. "That is a mighty fish tale. Or seal tale." He laughed again.

The boat rocked again, and Mr. Bingley gripped his cushion as they cut through the waves.

"What is?" Miss Bingley asked, rising from her brother's side where she had knelt, murmuring with him.

Miss Bingley started towards where Mr. Darcy and the others were gathering near the edge of the deck. Mr. Bingley called out, "Caroline! Come back!"

Mr. Darcy said, "Perhaps it would be best if we all join the others until we are in calmer waters."

Miss Elizabeth, to Darcy's gratitude, agreed, taking her sister's hand. "Come, Lydia. We do not wish to trouble our hosts."

Lydia glanced at Mr. Dunham who was steering the ship and occasionally called out to Mr. Whitmore who busied himself with the sails.

They rejoined the others in the center of the front, main deck where a pile of pillows sat atop a large, colorful tarp. Mr. Dunham called out something else to Mr. Whitmore, who pulled at one of the ropes. Wind buffeted Darcy's face and hair as the sailboat turned.

When the maneuver was complete, the boat moved parallel to the shoreline, far enough to avoid rocks and shallows, but close enough to track along the shore as the scene shifted from houses to green.

Mr. Stanton stepped away from the sails at Mr. Dunham's call, and they conversed a minute longer. Mr. Stanton nodded and Mr. Dunham walked to the group. He addressed the ladies first, his gaze on Miss Bingley. "My, the sea air has cast a lovely hue to everyone's complexion. I trust our first leg was not too rocky?"

Mr. Bingley, still gripping the cushion beneath

him, said, "Who is directing the driving of the boat?"

"Mr. Whitmore, for now. He is an experienced seaman."

"Oh. That is reassuring."

Mr. Bingley, not following Mr. Darcy's advice, kept his gaze fixed on the deck in front of him. Darcy was tempted to ask Mr. Dunham for a bucket, but he would not embarrass his friend unless it became necessary.

Mr. Dunham pointed to a large chest which Mr. Bingley leaned back against. "We have refreshments inside, if you wish. I purchased an ice block, so they are chilled. Which do you prefer: juice, wine?"

Lydia perked up at the mention of wine, and Elizabeth said, "I believe it best we enjoy the wine with our picnic dinner."

Mr. Dunham said, "Yes of course. Juice then."

Lydia glared at Elizabeth.

Elizabeth ignored her.

"Thank you all for joining me on this jaunt. I rarely get to share my love of boating with others. And I must admit, I was not completely forthright in my description of our trip."

"How so?" Mr. Darcy cut in. Did it have something to do with Mr. Dunham's exchange with Mr. Wickham?

Mr. Dunham laughed. "Nothing so dire as your expression, Mr. Darcy. There is a special place I hoped to show Miss Bingley, and all of you. It is accessible by foot, but would take an hour by carriage to visit."

"Oh, Mr. Dunham, do tell us more about this place." Miss Bingley clapped her hands, eyes bright and grinning like a child.

Darcy again wished he had not witnessed Mr. Dunham and Wickham's conversation. Perhaps it was harmless. Perhaps Mr. Wickham had somehow convinced Mr. Dunham he possessed information he did not, for a fee of course, and Mr. Dunham was just as much of a dupe as Mr. Bingley's other "friends."

Before leaving, Mr. Darcy had made inquiries with some officers who had taken their breakfast in the hotel dining area. All had been surprised at the notion a man working in records would have information about ocean currents.

"Better to talk to one of the older fishermen," one gentleman had said, looking up from his sausage for a moment before returning his attention, sawing off another hunk and popping it into his mouth with an appreciative 'hmmm'.

Even the servants of the hotel had, at Mr. Darcy's questions of where one might find this information, offered many suggestions with whom he could speak, none associated with militia records.

Lydia asked, "Well then, what is it?"

"A surprise."

Though the sea had calmed some since their changing direction to follow the shoreline, Bingley's face was still pale, and he sweated, swallowing occasionally, his eyes half shut.

Bingley leaned forward off the chest, and Mr. Darcy joined Mr. Dunham in lifting the cover. Inside, atop a block of ice, lay containers of juice, water, white wine and cool tea and several closed containers of what looked like foods. Mr. Dunham said, "Cold meats and cheese. There's bread in the storage hold."

Mr. Stanton rifled through a basket next to the chest and handed out heavy glasses. The boat turned from shore, rocking again, and Mr. Bingley jumped to his feet and rammed to the railing, leaning over. He retched.

Mr. Dunham said, "My apologies. I did not know you were inclined towards seasickness."

Miss Bingley walked to her brother's side and rested her palm on his back.

Mr. Dunham said, "I hope you do not need us to turn back to shore."

Miss Bingley, her voice firm and loud, said, "My brother will be fine. The apothecary gave him draughts."

If Mr. Bingley had visited an apothecary, the man had failed this day in his craft.

Mr. Darcy, not liking the exchange between Mr. Wickham and Mr. Dunham, and further disliking surprises, said, "Bingley, if we must return, then—"

"No, Darcy. My sister is correct."

Bingley's voice was stronger than it had been earlier, and he straightened, both hands on the deck rail. "I will improve, I think. I would not have my sister's trip ruined."

Mr. Stanton held out a glass. "Pour him some water and add a touch of whiskey. Do you have whiskey?"

Mr. Dunham shook his head.

Miss Lydia asked, "Is that a cure for seasickness?"

Mr. Stanton shrugged. "A touch of whiskey fixes

most of what ails me." He held out a glass as Darcy poured chilled water.

Mr. Stanton fiddled around in the inside pocket of his coat and took out a small flask. Before Darcy could protest, he tipped some of the contents inside of Bingley's cup. A whiff of spirits, blown over with the breeze, touched Darcy's nose. Mr. Stanton winked at Darcy, and standing, crossed the deck to Bingley and his sister.

Mr. Bingley took the glass and sniffed it, murmuring something to Mr. Stanton who, with a wave of his hand, encouraged Bingley to partake.

After another few seconds of consideration, Mr. Bingley did.

Mr. Stanton returned, settling himself on a cushion as Miss Lydia said, "Perhaps Mr. Bingley has suffered heartbreak?"

"The man is obviously ill for being on a boat, Lydia," Miss Elizabeth said.

"But does not heartbreak exhibit many of the same symptoms?" Lydia added, "Mr. Darcy, what do you think?"

Miss Elizabeth shot back, "I doubt Mr. Darcy has much knowledge of heartbreak."

How could Miss Elizabeth intimate Darcy did

not know of heartbreak, when she had broken his? He said, "I have knowledge of heartbreak."

Elizabeth refused to meet his eyes, staring down at the cushion upon which she sat, legs folded beside her. She fiddled with the gold rope running along the seam.

Lydia raised her eyebrows. "Have you? Is it, as they say, a disturbance of the gut? A painful twisting, a difficulty to breathe, is it any of those things?"

"Lydia, be quiet." Elizabeth still looked down at the cushion.

Mr. Stanton said, "A touch of whiskey is good for the heart, I've found. Perhaps a flask if the heartbreak is acute." He laughed.

Elizabeth asked, "How can one claim heartbreak when they do not know the object of their affections?"

"But Lizzy, who truly knows a person with whom they fall in love? They hardly allow a lady and gentleman time in each other's presence unchaperoned. It is through our small habits we know each other. Like sometimes, Lizzy, you whistle when you sleep."

"I do not!"

"You do! Through your teeth. It has often kept

me awake when I would have drifted off. But I don't blame you."

"You snore."

"Mary much prefers my snoring to Kitty's."

Everyone's snoring was preferable to Kitty's, who tossed, wheezed, and coughed through most nights.

Bingley and his sister stepped away from the deck. Bingley's color had improved, though he was still pale, half-full glass in hand. Miss Bingley linked her arm with his. Darcy shifted over, allowing his friend a place to sit between himself and the Bennet sisters.

Bingley sat.

Lydia said, "Mr. Bingley, you look improved."

Elizabeth said. "I am glad."

Miss Bingley asked, "What were you all discussing with such earnestness? We could hardly hear over the wind."

Miss Lydia said, "Heartbreak. Mr. Darcy was sharing his experience of it."

Miss Elizabeth said, "And it is not the conversation of a group enjoying a pleasure cruise."

Miss Bingley said, "I concur. Heartbreak?" Miss Bingley's eyes narrowed, and Darcy noted a glint of something, perhaps triumph, in her gaze. The left corner of her mouth twitched upwards.

But it was Bingley who unsettled Darcy the most. He asked, "Darcy? I had not realized a young lady had caught your eye. A distant heartbreak, I hope."

Darcy looked down at his hands. "I concur with Miss Bingley and Miss Elizabeth. Heartbreak is hardly an appropriate conversation for a jaunt such as this."

Mr. Dunham, after pouring Miss Bingley's glass with elderberry juice and serving himself, passed the bottle to Mr. Stanton who did the same, adding a touch of whiskey and then offering to pour for Miss Elizabeth who nodded and said, "Just juice."

Mr. Stanton did as requested and took a sip from his glass. "Wonderful, Dunham. Elizabeth poured Lydia's glass, and then passed it to Bingley and then Darcy.

Dunham said, "While heartbreak is an unfortunate fact of our existence, I much prefer the opposite. We risk heartbreak hoping our heart's desires will be met, and in that hope, one must risk failure."

Miss Bingley nodded. "I would not wish myself the cause of any man's heartbreak." She glanced again at Mr. Darcy.

Mr. Dunham, noting her gaze, said, "Miss Bingley, your beauty is alone enough any man might risk his heart to hope for such a reward."

Mr. Stanton said, "Mr. Dunham is quite the charmer."

Though the wind was strong, Miss Bingley reached into her purse and pulled out her peacock feather fan. Her cheeks had a light blush which could as well be attributed to the whipping air as a lady's shyness or embarrassment.

Darcy glanced over to Mr. Whitmore who maneuvered the craft with single-minded focus.

Miss Bingley said, "I cannot claim myself worthy of such a compliment."

"Certainly, you can. Mr. Bingley?"

Bingley took another sip of his doctored water. "It is not proper for a man to judge his sister's beauty."

"Of course. Of course!"

Miss Bingley said, "And do not ask Mr. Darcy. He is not one for idle compliments."

Darcy, fairly certain she had insulted him, said, "All the ladies here are possessed of their own beauty, though as Miss Bingley says, I am not one to offer compliments for the sake of offering comments."

Miss Elizabeth took a breath and with a smile, strained around the edges, said, "I should like to know more of the sights we are viewing. It is my and Lydia's first visit to Brighton."

Darcy, recognizing an opportunity, said, "I hope this is not much off your usual route. Are the currents much variable in this area?"

Mr. Dunham cocked his head, his brows furrowing. Then he gave a minute nod, almost as though consulting with himself. "Sometimes," he said.

"I hope Mr. Whitmore is making good use of the information about the currents you requested."

Mr. Dunham swiped his hand over his knee. "Mr. Whitmore has studied it." He said.

"But he does not need it now?"

"The currents are as expected," Mr. Dunham said. "I merely wished to confirm our route."

Mr. Bingley, his smile affable as always, said, "For one, I am grateful. A safer journey suits me well." Bingley sipped at his whiskey-scented water. "How did you make Mr. Wickham's acquaintance?"

"At the card table. I rarely indulge in games of chance, but a friend from university is very fond, and I showed him the local clubs I knew. It was a game of Commerce, I believe. Mr. Wickham is adept. We conversed. He is fond of the sea. He said he would have liked to have been sent to the Navy as a boy to grow up on the waves and have grand adventures, but his father was loath to send him away."

Darcy gritted his teeth. Wickham had never envisioned the slightest interest in naval life when they were boys, excepting one game of Pirates where was King of the Pirates.

Bingley said "It is unfortunate for a boy to be denied his dreams."

"Unfortunate," Darcy said, not bothering to hide his skepticism. "We grew up together as boys, and I have no memory of his pining for a naval life."

"Mr. Dunham shrugged. "I do not know. It is what he told me. I cannot say we are close, Mr. Wickham and I. I mentioned my desire to sail along the coastline, and he offered his assistance. Forgive my boldness, but it did not seem to me you are close with Mr. Wickham. He did not mention you at all. But again, I cannot claim to know him well."

"We are not close," Darcy confirmed.

Everything about Mr. Dunham's story was plausible. He was likely the victim of one of Wickham's schemes. Miss Bingley would do better than to marry a dupe, no matter how infatuated the pair appeared with each other. But Darcy would need to discover how Mr. Dunham had been duped, otherwise it was all supposition. And Darcy had made the same mistake with Bingley. He would not upset another Bingley's life without a better reason than 'I find him suspicious.'

Mr. Dunham called everyone's attention again to the coastline and a series of small cottages along the shore. Bingley met Darcy's eye and with one shoulder, shrugged.

The conversation turned to the landscape, with Mr. Dunham crinkling occasional compliments to Miss Bingley, and to a lesser degree, the other ladies. His preference was clear, and Miss Bingley's wide smile and the hint of blush on her cheeks showed how well she appreciated the attention.

The ship turned from the shoreline to deeper waters. Bingley, nervous, asked, "Why are we heading out to sea?"

Mr. Dunham said, "No reason to worry. The waters are too shallow in this area to pass safely, and it is best to go out until the waters deepen again.

Bingley nodded.

Mr. Stanton suggested a game of cards, to which the others agreed. Thus they passed another half an hour in idle repartee.

Lydia was, as usual, far more interested in idle conversation than the cards in her hand, and quickly, if cheerfully, lost every game.

The boat turned back towards shore. Mr. Dunham stood. "We are almost here." He waved to Mr. Whitmore, who steered to turn the boat into what looked like a half circle with a long bit of land jutting at the far end to form a point.

Miss Bingley, standing, let out a gasp as she looked to the shore which was swathed in a cloak of green and speckled lavender.

"Oh, Mr. Dunham!" Miss Lydia said, clasping her hands together above her bosom. "How lovely!"

Darcy did not fault Dunham his choice of destination. It was beautiful, and Darcy allowed his suspicions to recede as he glanced at Miss Elizabeth, who had also stood, eyes wide. She sniffed at the air and said, "I can smell it."

"Sometimes, when the wind blows to sea, you can."

Miss Lydia said, "The water is so still. I should love to take a dip."

Mr. Dunham shook his head. "I would fear for your safety without a dipper present to supervise bathing."

"My bathing is well enough, though perhaps Elizabe—"

"I may not be as adept as you, Lydia, but provided there are no harsh currents, I can swim well enough."

Ignoring her sister, Lydia asked, "May we at least dip our feet? Mrs. Forster would be most amenable."

Mrs. Forster attempted a measured tone, but her gaze flitted to the stern and said, "I should find it very pleasant."

Dunham nodded. "Once we are anchored, bathe your toes as you wish."

The anchor was lowered, and Lydia and Mrs. Forster sat and dipped their toes. Miss Elizabeth followed, though instead of bathing, she stood and looked out to the shore. Darcy remained with the others. Mr. Stanton suggested another hand of cards. The others agreed, and they played for a while.

As Mr. Stanton was dealing the third hand, Lydia called out, "Look, another boat!"

Had Darcy not been looking at Dunham, he would have missed the parting of the man's lips and a subtle relaxation of his shoulders and expression. Relief? Dunham stood. "Good. Captain Martín owes me six cases of wine." He pronounced the captain's name with a Spanish accent. Perhaps the *Lucia Itzel* was out of Spain and not England. Not that it much mattered. The two nations were allied now against the French. "Mr. Stanton, prepare the rope."

The older gentleman showed no annoyance at being ordered about so, instead grabbing a large spool of rope. Mr. Whitmore hurried up from under the main deck with three, leather-wrapped bumpers. A rope was tied to the top of each. He ran to the side of the hull and tied each so that they hung down at the widest part of the hull.

Darcy asked, "We are inviting them aboard?"

"We will tie together for a short time," Mr. Dunham said.

"Is that safe?" Bingley asked.

"Quite," Dunham said. "As I said, Captain Martín owes me six cases of wine."

"Not French, I hope!" Mrs. Hurst exclaimed.

Mr. Dunham flinched. "Spanish," he said. "We are not at war with Spain."

"Not currently," Mrs. Hurst said.

The *Lucia Itzel* sailed closer.

# CHAPTER 16

E lizabeth leaned on her elbows and gazed over the edge of the deck to a finger of land reaching to the sea. It was peaceful here. The water made a pleasant lapping sound against the hull, and except for Lydia's overly loud laughter and Mrs. Forster's occasional counterpoint, the area was serene. A pair of birds drifted over the outcropping of land, wings outstretched above. Clouds, white, fluffy masses that reminded Elizabeth of clean, sheared wool. The air smelled of salt, but when the wind shifted, it brought a touch of lavender.

"Your earring!" Mrs. Forster plucked at the shoulder of Lydia's frock, pulling free an angelskin coral earring.

"Oh!" Lydia exclaimed, feeling at her bare earlobe.

Lydia, in a surfeit of foolishness, had worn the earrings and a matching light-pink necklace. Both were gifts from Mrs. Bennet, who had loaned them to Lydia for their trip. Mrs. Bennet had offered no jewelry to Elizabeth, not that Elizabeth much minded except for her mother's dismissive statement, "Lizzy, I know you have no interest in flirting." An excuse offered as an explanation that only reminded Elizabeth how little her mother favored her.

Ordinarily, Elizabeth ignored her mother's slights. Elizabeth and her father were close, and she preferred his jests and love of reading to her mother's unending gossip and discussions of fashion. But the gift of jewelry, or the lack of it, had stung.

Elizabeth had suggested Lydia leave the jewelry at Mrs. Forster's, which had only made the girl more determined to wear it.

No matter. If Lydia chose to be careless, it was on Lydia's head.

Elizabeth shut her eyes and let the sun kiss her face. They drifted a while. Mrs. Forster and Lydia chatted and Elizabeth ignored them until Lydia called out. "Look! The other boat has arrived!"

Elizabeth gave a start and turned. The second sailboat turned into the harbor. Perhaps they would stay to join them for dinner and to enjoy the sunset.

Lydia pulled her feet from the water.

The *Lucia Itzel* was longer than the *Artemis* by ten feet, with taller sails. As the *Lucia Itzel* came closer, Elizabeth noted a young man, short and thin with short sleeves and weathered trousers, climbing through the rigging.

Mr. Dunham crossed the edge of the deck and waved to them with a long sweep of his right arm. Elizabeth, curious, walked to him as, on the opposite boat, a dark-haired man with a weathered face called out. The wind stole his voice, but Mr. Dunham must have understood because he waved the boat closer.

Mr. Darcy joined them with Miss Bingley, leaving her brother alone in the middle of the deck amidst the abandoned cushions. Miss Bingley said to Mr. Dunham, "You are certain this is safe?"

"Absolutely," Mr. Dunham said. "It is a common thing when one happens across an old friend at sea."

Perhaps it was. Elizabeth, beyond reading her father's newspapers and the evidence of an occasional novel, she did not know what one did or did not do while sailing.

Lydia made her way over and squinted as best she could, likely hoping one of the men might be handsome and open to flirting. Though what joy Lydia would have in flirting with a group of Spanish sailors, Elizabeth could not understand.

Though the *Lucia Itzel* was a bit taller than the *Artemis*, they were close enough for Mr. Stanton to toss a rope across. The young man in the rigging scurried down and snatched up the rope and tied it to the bow of his own boat. Mr. Whitmore repeated the same task at the stern, and then both sides threw the rope over again, this time forming an X along the middle. Though the water was calm, the boats still rose and fell, occasionally knocking into the leather-clad bumpers.

Once the two boats were tied together, Mr. Dunham said, "If you'll excuse me a moment," and climbed over to the other boat.

Elizabeth glanced at Mr. Darcy. "Have you sailed before? And if so, is this as ordinary as Mr. Dunham suggests?"

Mr. Darcy said, "No. They put my cousin on the ship to return to the front, but that was a naval ship, and their purpose was war, not pleasure and a friendly chat." Mr. Darcy's expression was grim. Of course, Mr. Darcy's expression was often grim. He had a fine mastery of the grim expression.

Lydia asked, "Do you think the *Lucia Itzel*'s captain will allow us aboard if we ask?"

"No! Even if they allowed it, it is wholly improper to pay call to a ship full of strange foreign men.

Lydia said, "I suppose."

"Your sister is correct." Mr. Darcy said.

Lydia let out a snort. "You would say that."

Elizabeth glanced at Mr. Darcy who shrugged.

Mr. Dunham stood on the opposite deck, having a rapid conversation with the other captain. The wind and distance made it so Elizabeth could only make out the occasional word. Most were in Spanish. Elizabeth, who had barely studied French, could not make heads or tails of it. But the conversation did not appear friendly. It was not contentious, merely serious. Odd for two men who had shared such a friendly relationship they needed to stop, mid-cruise, to pay greetings to one other.

"Do you think he will invite Captain Martín aboard?"

"Perhaps."

Miss Bingley clutched the railing and leaned

forward as though the few extra inches might give her a better understanding of what Mr. Dunham and his acquaintance were discussing. "I can hardly make out a word they are saying."

Lydia said, "I do not believe they are speaking English."

"Of course not. It is Spanish."

You speak Spanish, Miss Bingley?" Lydia asked.

Miss Bingley, taking her gaze away from the conversation on the neighboring boat, looked down her nose at Lydia and asked, "You do not?"

Though Lydia was often irritating, Elizabeth wanted to defend her sister. Unfortunately, she could not claim Lydia or she, herself, possessed Miss Bingley's refined education. After returning from her dinner at Netherfield, Jane had mentioned Miss Bingley having attended seminary school.

Before Elizabeth could plan a clever response, the Spanish captain said something, and he either spoke more loudly or, more likely, the wind shifted, and a snatch of the conversation carried over, and Miss Bingley cocked her head.

"Bottles?" she murmured.

Elizabeth asked, "They are discussing bottles? I suppose it is the wine Mr. Martín owes him."

"I suppose."

The captain waved Mr. Dunham away from the deck's edge. They walked towards the ship's main sail. The captain knelt. After a moment, Mr. Dunham stepped down, below the sailboat's deck.

"I suppose he is getting the wine," Miss Bingley mused.

Elizabeth could only presume the same thing. Except if this was a meeting by chance, how had Captain Martín known to bring the wine he owed Mr. Dunham?

Elizabeth glanced at Mr. Darcy who stood, eyes narrowed, fingers clasped behind his back.

The two men returned, now smiling, and Mr. Dunham hopped back to the *Artemis* while the captain called out orders to his men, two of whom scrambled towards the open hatch in the center of their deck.

"Thank you for your patience," Mr. Dunham said. "Captain Martín has not only the wine he promised, but chocolate sweets."

"Oh! I hope we can have a taste."

Miss Bingley glared at Lydia again. "I do not believe it is our place to impose, considering the kindness Mr. Dunham has shown in allowing us to accompany him on his trip."

"Nonsense," Mr. Dunham said. "Though it is a

testament to your kind spirit, you take such care not to be an imposition, Miss Bingley."

Miss Bingley cast her gaze down and with an artful glance up through her lashes said, "I thank you for the compliment, though much appreciated I cannot say it is deserved."

The treacle of Mr. Dunham and Miss Bingley's flirtations was enough to set Elizabeth off sweets forever.

Capt. Martín stepped onto the deck. Mr. Dunham made introductions. The captain bowed. "My pleasure to meet you," he said in heavily accented English.

The Spanish captain was a rugged and, if Elizabeth was honest with herself, attractive gentleman, whose weathered face seemed somewhere in its fourth decade. His jaw was close shaven, and he had a mustache, dark brown with a few strands of salted white. He wore a wool coat, a ruffled shirt, hemp pantaloons and well-worn boots.

"My men…" Capt. Martín looked back at the ship and waved to the gentlemen, each carrying a wooden crate "…will see goods to your hold."

Mr. Whitmore met with two men with crates and guided them down a set of stairs to the small hold. Elizabeth remembered from Mr. Dunham's brief tour of the boat that the below-deck hold held two small compartments for storage.

Miss Bingley curtsied and greeted him in Spanish. Capt. Martín's eyes widened, and his gaze flitted to Mr. Dunham who raised his shoulders slightly.

With a smile, Capt. Martín said something to Miss Bingley which made her take out her fan and flutter it at her face.

Mr. Bingley, who had, at some point during their conversation, got himself upright and walked to the group, Mrs. Hurst at his side, said "Mr. Dunham, are we having your friend for dinner?"

"No, sir," Captain Martín said. "I had only…to settle…debt with Mr. Dunham."

Mr. Dunham said, "A friendly wager, that was all. A race. We had a race. Captain Martín thought his boat faster with larger sails, but Mr. Whitmore here, along with myself, pushed ahead by a nose."

"How exciting!" Lydia said with a clap of her hands. "How did you meet? Was it on the open sea?"

That had to be the most ridiculous question Elizabeth could have imagined. If she could imagine such a question. She said, "How would they have met? Are sailors much in the habit of stopping for conversation in their travels?"

Capt. Martín's lips twitched. "If they have promise of such beauty and wit before me, yes."

His English improved in flattery, Elizabeth thought. But they said sailors do have reputations as flirts.

Capt. Martín held out a single bottle of wine and a small, canvas sack. He said, "For you, to guests." He handed the bottle to Mr. Dunham who smiled and thanked him.

Mr. Dunham handed the bottle to Miss Bingley, who looked over the label and smiled. "Fine vintage," she said, adding something else in Spanish which made Capt. Martín smile.

"*Gracias*. I must take leave."

Miss Bingley said, "You are not staying for dinner?"

"I must be off. But if I—time for you—" Capt. Martín followed up with something in Spanish that made Miss Bingley blush.

Mr. Darcy's expression tightened, his lips pressing together and his eyes narrowing.

Was Mr. Darcy jealous? He had shown no interest in Miss Bingley at Netherfield, but a man's interests could change.

Or, Capt. Martín had said something unseemly. In which case, Mr. Darcy had understood it.

It did not surprise Elizabeth that Mr. Darcy spoke Spanish. His education must have been at least as good as Miss Bingley's.

Mr. Dunham said something in Spanish to the captain, who laughed. Mr. Darcy did not look amused.

Mr. Dunham said something else, more sharply, and the captain, this time in English, said, "I meant no offense; if you will allow me to take my leave."

Though still accented, the captain's English had improved. Elizabeth glanced again at Mr. Darcy, but the man's expression did not change.

With that, the captain and his two shipmates returned to the *Lucia Itzel*. The captain called out something in Spanish and the men on deck began untying their boat.

Mr. Dunham said, "I will save these sweets for after our meal."

Lydia opened her mouth to protest, and Elizabeth gave her a firm elbow in the side. "A fine idea," Elizabeth said. "And we are most grateful to you for sharing your treat."

"Yes," Lydia said, remembering her manners. "Most grateful."

Lydia and Mrs. Forster went to the stern of the boat with Mr. Dunham who began untying one of the lines while Mr. Whitmore managed the other. Miss Bingley followed Mr. Dunham as Mr. Bingley returned to the cushions with Mrs. Hurst, allowing Mr. Darcy and Elizabeth a moment to themselves.

Elizabeth glanced at Mr. Darcy, who stared out at the *Lucia Itzel*, his lips tight. He suspected something. Elizabeth stepped closer to him, leaning her elbows on the rail, looking out at the other ship. She said, voice pitched low, "What troubles you?"

"Nothing."

The sleeves of Elizabeth's dress were short, exposing a patch of skin between the base of the sleeve and the topmost edge of her glove. It rested against the linen of Mr. Darcy's jacket. He smelled of sweat and sandalwood, and Elizabeth wished to lean closer, craving the mix of it with the salt of the sea.

Elizabeth asked, "Do you speak Spanish?"

"Enough," Mr. Darcy said.

It was on the tip of Elizabeth's tongue to ask why Darcy had kept his ability to himself, but he was not one for idle conversation. Or maybe he suspected something more than a friendly bet. Elizabeth agreed. She wondered what it would take to get a look inside of one of the crates. "Do you think it is as he said? Wine?"

"They were discussing bottles."

"Hmm..."

"Do not think of it."

"Bottles?"

"Going below deck."

Elizabeth's breath caught. How had she given herself away? "What makes you believe I would do such a thing?"

"My judgment of character is not always in error." Mr. Darcy smiled, and Elizabeth's breath caught again. He was a different man when he smiled. The corners of his eyes crinkled, and his features softened.

Mr. Bingley, back at the cushions, called out, "Darcy, step back! It is dangerous to be so near the edge when these boats are being untied."

"Is it?"

"At least have a care for Miss Elizabeth's safety."

Darcy's smile faded, to Elizabeth's dismay. He said, "I always have a care for your safety, Miss Elizabeth."

Mr. Darcy held out his arm, and Elizabeth took it, wishing her enjoyment of their closeness was not a betrayal.

Once the boats were untied, the *Lucia Itzel* pulled away, picking up speed as it turned back to the channel.

Mrs. Forester and Lydia returned at the stern, bare feet dangling. Miss Bingley asked about another round of cards, and they played. Elizabeth wondered again at the crates. She could think of no way to get herself below the deck. The hatch sat in plain view, and she had no reason to go there. As much as it galled her, Mr. Darcy was correct. Elizabeth would be better to let the incident go. If Miss Bingley wished to court with a smuggler, it was her affair. Elizabeth had no business interfering. For once, Miss Bingley seemed to have all well in hand.

With that, Elizabeth looked down at her cards.

# CHAPTER 17

**M**r. Darcy had to get into one of those crates. If it was Spanish wine, as Mr. Dunham had said, then a quick look would verify the contents and Mr. Darcy's conscience would be appeased. But with Wickham involved, Darcy suspected the contents of the crates were more problematic. Something dangerous.

Darcy did not much care if Mr. Dunham was trying to avoid paying duties for himself. It was a common crime, if avoiding the excessive taxes imposed by Parliament could even be considered a crime.

But if Mr. Dunham intended to sell, it gave him more dangerous acquaintances. The sort who would endanger more than Miss Bingley's reputation, maybe even her life.

After a few hands, Mr. Dunham invited Miss Bingley to observe the shore from the side of the deck, remarking sometimes when the sea was still, one might witness sea turtles, dolphins, and the occasional seal.

Mrs. Hurst and Mr. Stanton joined them while Mr. Whitmore took his place again at the wheel, which left Darcy and Bingley a moment to themselves.

Bingley said, "I admit, I was doubtful at first, but Mr. Dunham is besotted with my sister and she him."

"The incident with the *Lucia Itzel* does not concern you?" Mr. Darcy ventured.

"The duties on wine are crushing, and perhaps he wished to avoid them. It is a crime, but not one of great import." Bingley said, "Miss Lydia seems to think her sister has lingering feelings for me."

"That is not what she said."

"Perhaps not, but if Miss Jane missed me…" Bingley shook his head. "Even if she had, I'm certain she has moved her attention to another. It has been months. We made no promises to each other, and I fled most abruptly."

Now was the time to confess. Bingley was not paying much mind to Darcy's reservations about Mr. Dunham, and the weight of Darcy's secret made it difficult to view anything objectively. He second-guessed himself at every turn. Worse, he second-guessed his second guesses. If he had been wrong about Jane, he could be wrong about Dunham. A conversation and a handing over of a single sheet of paper was hardly reason to break a courtship. Had Darcy not rendered judgment against Miss Jane Bennet with even less evidence?

Darcy's gaze drifted over to Miss Elizabeth, who unlike Mrs. Forster and Miss Lydia, did not dip her feet over the side of the boat but stood, with her elbows on the rails, looking out at sea. Haloed in the sun, she seemed a fanciful creature of legend rather than an ordinary Miss. Though how any deem Miss Elizabeth ordinary was beyond Darcy's comprehension. How had he once declared her merely tolerable?

Darcy, who had always prided himself on his quick and accurate judgment, knew himself to be a fraud. He said, "Bingley, there's something I must tell you."

Bingley looked over at his friend. "By that

expression, one might expect you to confess to a murder, Darcy." Bingley smiled.

Darcy could not. "I have wronged you," Darcy said.

It was because Darcy deserved the ire of the Gods, that at that moment, Mr. Dunham with Miss Bingley on his arm, started back towards them.

"Darcy, what is it?" Bingley asked. "Surely it cannot be a murder?"

"No," Darcy said.

"Charles! You are looking much less peaked," Miss Bingley called out to her brother.

Darcy said, "Later. We will speak later."

"Darcy, you are my closest friend. Whatever harm you believe you have done, I forgive you."

Bingley, kind and loyal to his core. Darcy did not deserve the man's friendship, and once they were alone and Darcy had confessed, he feared he would lose it.

"Charles?" Miss Bingley said with a smile. "I trust you two are not discussing heartbreak again. This is supposed to be a pleasure cruise."

Dunham said, "The company has been a pleasure for me."

Bingley smiled, but Darcy noted a tension in him. He had offered Darcy forgiveness, and now, perhaps he doubted himself. Darcy could not blame Bingley for his doubts.

Bingley said, "Darcy has not confessed heart-break. Only his misgivings about the wine."

Mr. Dunham paled. "Misgivings?"

"We have not sampled it, so how can we assess if the good Captain Martín offered you a proper payout for your wager?"

"Is that all?" Dunham laughed, "I suppose it can do little harm to sample the wine before our repast. If you do not find it objectionable, Miss Bingley."

Miss Bingley said, "We had best call Louisa over. She is fond of wine, especially the Spanish vintages."

Miss Bingley glanced back the way they had come. Mrs. Hurst and Mr. Stanton stood close, speaking. Mr. Stanton leaned one elbow on the ship's rail and nodded, his pipe hanging from the side of his mouth. Mrs. Hurst said something, and he nodded again.

"Louisa!" Miss Bingley called to her sister, who looked up.

Mr. Stanton took the pipe from his mouth, placed it in the pocket of his jacket, and bowed.

Mrs. Hurst nodded, and lifting her skirts, started across the deck, Mr. Stanton a step behind.

Miss Bingley said, "I should think Miss Lydia is too young to indulge."

Darcy would've agreed, but neither his nor Miss Bingley's opinion much mattered since the girl was out. Again, Darcy wondered at Mr. and Mrs. Bennet's raising of their five daughters. Miss Elizabeth had turned out well, despite her upbringing. And though Darcy objected to Mr. Bingley's courtship with Miss Jane Bennet, the young woman possessed a gentility of spirit and manners that made her appealing. Perhaps Miss Lydia would grow into some semblance of propriety. Darcy doubted it, but beyond his own sister, who had been given the best governesses and tutors, Darcy did not have much experience with other young ladies.

Miss Lydia, leaning back on her hands and twisting at her waist, asked, "Is it dinner already?"

Both girls had lifted their skirts to their knees to not dampen them when boat rocked, and dipped their feet into the water.

Elizabeth turned and followed Miss Lydia and Mrs. Forster, who leapt up with childlike enthusiasm, and after stopping a moment to pick up their shoes, padded barefoot across the deck.

In contrast to the two young women, Mr. Stanton ambled, and he appeared to favor his left leg. The younger women had settled themselves by the time Mr. Stanton, now three steps behind Mrs. Hurst, lowered himself onto a cushion, hissing through his teeth as he sat. Mr. Stanton said, "Dunham, we may wish to start back early. My knee is telling me there may be a storm."

Mrs. Hurst said, "Nonsense! My elbow always bothers me when there is rain. I sprained it when I was a child, chasing a firefly, would you believe? I tripped. It was the worst pain of my life!" Mrs. Hurst declared.

Mr. Stanton said, "I cannot speak to your weather elbow, Mrs. Hurst. But my knee has never made a liar of me at sea."

Mr. Bingley said, "If you think there is to be a storm, let us turn back now."

Darcy looked out toward the horizon. The air was calm, and he noted no darkness either towards the sea or to the shore to show an oncoming storm.

Mr. Stanton said, "Mr. Dunham, you understand, it is not just the rains but the tides."

This made no sense to Darcy, but Dunham nodded. "Yes. The tides. They shift."

Seamen as capable as Mr. Dunham and Mr.

Whitmore, who had done the bulk of the sailing this afternoon, ought to understand the working of tides.

Dunham said, "Let us eat now."

"I am hungry now," Mrs. Hurst said. "How quickly does your knee offer you a warning of the weather? Is it an hour or day?"

"It varies," Mr. Stanton said. "I am certain we have a little time for our meal."

Bingley said, "Or we can start back and eat on your dock, Dunham. I have no fondness for storms, and if I must weather one, I'd rather have both my feet firmly on land."

"If it is not too much of a disappointment to Miss Bingley. I promised her a meal on the sea."

"My sister can eat just as well on land," Bingley declared.

Miss Elizabeth said, "If we were to observe the sunset over dinner, it would necessitate our returning in darkness, would it not?"

Miss Bingley bit her bottom lip. "Yes. I suppose. Let us eat now and return before that eventuality."

They ate. It was a pleasant enough meal. Though Dunham poured Miss Lydia only a small amount of wine, the young lady became tipsy, her laughter too loud and her hands far too expressive.

Lydia fiddled with her earring as she said, "It does not smell like rain. Is your knee always correct?"

Mrs. Hurst said, "My elbow is." She extended her arm, finger slightly curled and then lifted it, touching her fingers to her shoulder as she said, "I feel nothing."

The wine was good and the meal pleasant enough, though as they ate, Miss Lydia grew more and more affected by the wine, which made her laugh at inappropriate moments.

She extended her glass for a second serving, and Elizabeth placed her hand on top of it. "Have more meat," she insisted.

"But Lizzy!" Miss Lydia whined.

"I believe my sister has had enough, is that right, Mrs. Forster?" Elizabeth smiled, but her dark eyes were steely and her tone brokered no argument.

Mrs. Forster leaned back and said, "Dearest Lydia, we have only one bottle. Let everyone enjoy."

Miss Lydia laughed again. "There are six crates of wine, are there not? Let's have another!"

Elizabeth said, "We do not wish to inconvenience Mr. Dunham. Also, he will need his wits about him to steer us home."

Mr. Dunham said, "Quite right. We shall need the wine in our stores for our next dinner."

Mrs. Hurst asked, "Your renovations are almost finished then?"

Mr. Dunham nodded.

"We are most excited for when you will be ready to entertain guests," Mrs. Hurst continued. "These renovations have been a trial, taking so many of your days and evenings."

Miss Bingley glanced at her sister and pressed her lips together. She leaned closer to Mr. Dunham, not so much as to break the bounds of propriety, but with a certain affection. She said, "We are all grateful for your hospitality, bringing us today out on your boat. Louisa does not mean to imply you have been inhospitable."

Mr. Dunham smiled. "I have never thought her words a criticism," Mr. Dunham said. He piled two slices of meat onto his bread and, folding it, took a bite.

Miss Bingley speared her meat with a fork and with as much delicacy as she could manage, chewed slowly and then swallowed.

Miss Elizabeth, with less delicacy, took a slice of

beef and put the entire piece in her mouth, following up with a slice of bread and a sip of wine.

As they ate, Bingley grew more and more nervous. "Are the winds picking up?"

Miss Bingley said, "The wind is fine, Charles."

They finished the wine. Once the plates and the remains of the meal were put away, Lydia asked, "Have we time for sweets?"

Dunham smiled, his eyes twinkling. "Mr. Stanton."

"Yes. Yes."

A plate of sliced seasonal fruits was their dessert. After uncovering it, Mr. Dunham took the small, paper-wrapped package Capt. Martín had given him, and placed along the edge of the plate two dozen flat, chocolate disks sprinkled with white nonpareils.

Elizabeth's mouth watered at the treat. They quickly devoured their dessert.

Mr. Whitmore, who had said little through the afternoon, only nodding and giving one-word answers when addressed directly, stood. He walked to the ship's stern and started to wind up the anchor.

Mr. Darcy said, "Mr. Whitmore's very fond of sailing,"

Mr. Dunham nodded. "He was very distraught when he lost his boat."

"I am surprised he did not purchase another," Bingley said.

Dunham lowered his voice. "Mr. Whitmore has come upon hard times. It is best not to mention it, as he finds it distressing.

Miss Bingley swallowed, tapping her moist fingertips to a handkerchief before saying, "Poor Mr. Whitmore. We shall not mention his change in circumstances."

"Both he and I thank you," Mr. Dunham said solemnly.

Once again, though there was nothing objectionable about Mr. Dunham's story, it seemed odd to Darcy. Mr. Whitmore did not act like a young gentleman fallen on hard times. His manners were more of a servant. Even now, while the rest of them enjoyed sweets, he made adjustments to the sails, testing the wind with his fingers and once climbing up to alter the ropes.

But, if Mr. Whitmore was Dunham's servant, why the ruse? Perhaps Dunham did not know as much about sailing as he pretended, and he had brought Mr. Whitmore on to make up for his lack?

Again, Darcy wished to believe this charitable

explanation, but there was the issue of the crates and Mr. Wickham.

After they had docked and departed, perhaps Darcy could steal back and...

His own thoughts shocked him.

Sneaking onto another man's boat and rifling through his possessions was not the act of a gentleman.

But did he not owe Bingley and his sister for their friendship?

Darcy was not a man used to navigating shades of gray. He glanced at Miss Elizabeth, who had finished her dessert and taken a surreptitious lick of her fingers. Miss Lydia leaned back against the trunk, her legs crossed at her ankles, eyes half shut.

No head for wine, which Darcy supposed was to her credit though she acted the fool now.

If Darcy were a different man, and Miss Elizabeth a different woman, he might ask her advice. Miss Elizabeth seemed more comfortable than he was operating outside the bounds of what society required of her.

He must have stared a moment too long because Miss Elizabeth glanced over at him, and her brows lowered.

Darcy averted his gaze.

Dunham agreed it was time to return, and with a nod to Mr. Whitmore who once again took the wheel, the boat sailed from the cove.

The wind strengthened on the return journey, though perhaps it was only the direction they traveled. They reached the dock just before sunset.

Dunham thanked them all again.

Mr. Dunham said, "If my parlor were not in such disarray, I would invite you in for a visit."

Darcy glanced over at Mr. Dunham's townhouse. Whatever renovations were happening must have been on the inside. No equipment or materials were in view for outside restorations.

After they exchanged more pleasantries, Mrs. Forster, Lydia, and Miss Elizabeth made to their waiting carriage.

Dunham had sent his own carriage to retrieve Darcy, Mrs. Hurst and the Bingleys this morning.

Mr. Dunham said, "My carriage will be ready in a few minutes. We expected to return later, so I suppose that is why it is not already waiting."

Miss Bingley said, "It is no matter. We are happy to enjoy your company a while longer."

Bingley said, "I am on land and yet it is still rocking."

Miss Bingley remarked, "Perhaps it is the wine."

Darcy glanced back at the boat. Mr. Whitmore and Mr. Stanton were still aboard. Darcy asked, "Are they not coming?"

"Mr. Whitmore is very particular about the maintenance of the ship," Mr. Dunham said.

Further reinforcing the idea that these two men were servants and not gentlemen. Or at least Mr. Whitmore was a servant. Mr. Stanton acted more the gentleman, though he was also quick to follow orders. Perhaps he was a better actor. Or perhaps he had been raised in privilege but unable to claim a bloodline of his own.

Miss Bingley said, "I hope we can say our good-byes and give our thanks, especially to Mr. Whitmore, for such a smooth journey."

Mr. Dunham said, "They will be along.

Darcy, to gauge Mr. Dunham's reaction, said, "Why not have a servant attend to the boat so we can say our cordial goodbyes, as Mr. Whitmore and Mr. Stanton were as much your guests as we were?"

Mr. Dunham brushed his hand over the forearm of his jacket as though removing a speck of dirt. Darcy suspected the gesture was more to avert his gaze than grooming.

Mr. Dunham said, "Yes. If you will excuse me." He bowed and hurried towards the *Artemis*.

Bingley said, "I wonder when the earth will settle."

Miss Bingley, to her credit, took her brother's arm and said, "I am sorry, Charles. I had not realized— I knew you found sea travel distasteful, but I had thought a short sailing jaunt would be... Less difficult. I was selfish."

"Nonsense, Caroline," Mrs. Hurst said. "The last time Charles was on a boat, he was nine. How were you to know he would have such a poor reaction as an adult?"

Bingley smiled and patted Miss Bingley on the hand. "I am glad to see you so happy, Caroline. But the next time you sail, please leave me on shore."

Darcy, recognizing Bingley would be of no help in convincing Caroline to reconsider Mr. Dunham as a suitor, asked, "What did you think of the *Lucia Itzel*?"

"Captain Martín was charming," Miss Bingley interjected. "A born flirt, him. I suppose Mr. Dunham is the same, though to his credit, I do not see him flirting with other ladies when I am about." In the orange-gray remains of sunset, Darcy could not gauge Miss Bingley's color well enough to know if she blushed, but he suspected she had.

No, Miss Bingley did not seem inclined towards

suspicion either. It is only Mr. Darcy and, to her credit, Miss Elizabeth, who read more into the situation than the explanation given.

Mr. Dunham returned with Mr. Whitmore and Mr. Stanton.

Miss Bingley curtsied. "Mr. Stanton, Mr. Whitmore, I am much pleased that the both of you could join us on this excursion. Mr. Whitmore, your dedication to piloting the craft has earned our deepest approbation."

"Indeed," Darcy said.

Mrs. Hurst said, "Perhaps there is something to your knee, Mr. Stanton. My elbow has begun aching"

Mr. Stanton grinned. One of his lower teeth, on the left, near the corner of his mouth was missing. The gap was only apparent a moment due to the wideness of Mr. Stanton's grin. He said, "It is only that my knee is better adapted to gauging the weather on water, I believe."

Bingley said, "I, for one am happy for your warning. Better we arrive in port with the storm far at our rear than to battle it on the open water." With his usual informality, Bingley clapped Mr. Stanton on the shoulder.

Mr. Stanton, unperturbed, said, "It pleases me to be useful."

Mr. Dunham's carriage, pulled by a pair of solid, brown geldings, pulled around to the front.

Miss Bingley curtsied again. "Mr. Dunham, this day has been a joy. I cannot thank you enough for inviting us to join you."

"The reward was your smile and the light in your eyes as you saw something beautiful." Mr. Dunham took her hand and lifted, not quite pressing a kiss to her knuckles but enough to make clear, once again, his approbation.

A footman climbed down from the back and pulled open the door. The footman's clothing was pressed, and his shoes shined, but as Darcy passed, he noted worn fabric on the coat sleeves, which were short for the length of the footman's arms.

It was not a sign of Dunham's limited means, as the footman may have borrowed the jacket from another servant for the evening, his original clothing being mended. The carriage itself was as well appointed as any of Mr. Dunham's station and expected wealth would be.

The footman closed the carriage door. As they turned away from Mr. Dunham's home, he waved

Mr. Whitmore and Mr. Stanton back to the sailboat.

Bingley leaned back, stretching his arms over his head until they tapped the ceiling. "A civilized conveyance, carriages and horseback." Bingley's shoulders cracked as clasped his hands behind his head and bent his elbows. Darcy leaned forward so as not to be poked.

"I must say, Mr. Dunham showed himself in every way a gentleman."

"Mr. Whitmore did the bulk of the sailing," Mrs. Hurst said.

"Our brother cannot sail, and we would not consider him less a gentleman. And Mr. Darcy…?"

"I can row," Darcy said.

"Yes, you have the pond at Pemberley," Bingley said.

Miss Bingley returned to outlining Mr. Dunham's virtues while her sister attempted, with limited success, to temper Miss Bingley's praise. As they spoke, Bingley leaned to Darcy, breath tickling Darcy's ear as he said, "Visit my rooms tonight. We will have a bit of Port and you can tell me what you have done that will upset me so."

# CHAPTER 18

Lydia and Mrs. Forster outlined every moment of the day with giddy enthusiasm.

Lydia sighed, "I should like to learn Spanish. Now that we and Spain are not at war, it would be a delight to converse with handsome Spanish officers."

Mrs. Forster wrinkled her nose. "I suppose. Though it seems disloyal."

"My father says the Spanish are much closer to us in temperament than the French."

Elizabeth recalled her father saying no such thing. Elizabeth did not put it past her sister to invent a memory out of whole cloth. Likely, she even believed it.

It was a short ride to Mr. Forster's home in Brighton. If not for propriety, Elizabeth would have preferred to walk, but given the short distance, at least by carriage, she would need only make conversation for a short time.

Elizabeth's attention returned to the crates. It seemed an odd coincidence Capt. Martín would owe Mr. Dunham six crates of wine and just happen upon him by chance.

Coincidences happened, and if Mr. Dunham made a habit of visiting that cove when he sailed, then perhaps it had been good fortune. But if there was something more, Elizabeth wanted to know. She was tired of playing the part of the chaperone, working without thanks to protect Lydia's virtue while pursuing few of her own interests. She had enjoyed the jaunt by sea, except for again, Lydia; but, more than the entertainments and chocolate, the mystery compelled her. Elizabeth said, "Do you believe it common for ships to meet at sea in such a manner?"

Mrs. Forster shrugged. "Mr. Forster prefers to leave naval affairs to the naval forces. I can claim no particular knowledge of what is ordinary at sea."

Neither could Elizabeth.

Mr. Darcy also suspected something. He had

warned Elizabeth from looking in the crates, which meant he saw some reason why one might make such an attempt.

If Elizabeth were a different woman and Mr. Darcy a different man, she would ask if he had any plans to search, and perhaps…

Elizabeth lips twitched an involuntary smile. Imagine herself and Mr. Darcy breaking into a gentleman's ship to rifle through his belongings? Ridiculous.

Lydia fingered her necklace. "How does one go about learning Spanish?"

"You would need a tutor," Elizabeth said. "We can speak with Papa." If Lydia occupied herself in learning Spanish, it would force her to take a moment from flirting and flipping through fashion plates. That, if nothing else, would be a virtue.

Elizabeth doubted Lydia would stick with lessons for more than a few attempts, but if Papa hired a tutor for all of them, maybe Elizabeth could learn Spanish. She enjoyed languages. She had sat in with Charlotte's tutors occasionally, and while Elizabeth's French grammar had left much to be desired, the governess had complimented Elizabeth on her pronunciation.

Beyond the question of the crates was the

deeper problem of Mr. Bingley's affection. Had he seemed wistful, at first, when Lydia mentioned Jane?

Perhaps.

Elizabeth again considered writing her sister. Considering Mr. Darcy's sabotage of Mr. Bingley and Jane's relationship, telling Jane of his presence in Brighton would only cause more pain. But Elizabeth hated keeping such a secret from her sister. Bad enough she had said nothing of the proposal, she compounded the sin by saying nothing of Mr. Bingley's presence here. She offered Jane no chance to win back his heart.

Elizabeth was as bad as Mr. Darcy had been, protecting people by making decisions in their stead.

No more. Tonight, she would write a letter to Jane and send it off first thing in the morning. With hope, after Elizabeth confessed, Jane would forgive.

Mrs. Forster and Lydia retired to the parlor to continue their conversation, while Elizabeth, pleading tiredness, returned to their room. She had finished penning the letter and opened a novel on her lap, though her mind was too full of her own thoughts to focus on the story when Lydia returned.

Lydia murmured a greeting and went to the vanity. "Oh!"

Elizabeth looked up. "What is it?"

"I— It is nothing. A mistake."

Lydia was not one who hid her emotions well. Her hand shook as she dropped a single earring into the small wooden box her mother had given her the jewelry in.

Elizabeth asked, "Your earring?"

"It must have fallen in the parlor. It must have!"

"You and Mrs. Forster were into the sherry again," Elizabeth said. She need not make it a question, the color on Lydia's cheeks and the wobble in her steps made it clear she had been drinking.

Lydia waved her hand in the air, narrowly avoiding slapping the mirror as she turned to Elizabeth. "Only a little," she said.

"You know Mama does not approve of us becoming drunk." It was one of Mrs. Bennet's few rules.

"I was not drunk in public; it was only with Mrs. Forster, my dear friend."

"And on the boat?"

"I only had a few sips."

Elizabeth sighed through her teeth. "Come along then, let us search the parlor."

"You do not have to go with me if you do not wish. I can search myself."

"With two pairs of eyes, the search will go faster, and it will be sooner for both of us to bed." Lydia's aching head in the morning would do more than any lecture to discourage her from further drunkenness.

"Well…" Lydia turned to the door. "As you wish then. But do not cast blame upon me. I did not ask for your help."

What was Elizabeth going to do with Lydia? They had but another fortnight in Brighton, and on nights like this, Elizabeth counted the days. But no matter her sister's protests, it would hurt both herself and their mother for Lydia to lose the jewelry.

Elizabeth took a lantern and, together, she and Lydia descended the stairs to the parlor. Col. Forster was possessed of some wealth but kept a modest home.

A pianoforte stood in the corner, the lid shut. The walls were papered in golden brocade, and an elaborate plasterwork was carved over the fireplace. Two large windows were positioned at one side of the room to allow a view of a small garden and let in the sea breezes. Another house obscured the sea, and though they were within walking distance of the Old Steyne, they were not so close as to be considered fashionable.

Elizabeth was glad for the distance from the main thoroughfares. It allowed her to sleep more easily and kept Lydia from witnessing excitements, in which she would then feel compelled to participate. This restricted her flirting to the daylight hours, assemblies, and the entertainments Mrs. Forster had organized.

A table with two padded chairs sat near the wall beside the pianoforte. Elizabeth lit a second lantern and placed it on the table. She asked, "Were you seated here?"

Lydia nodded and dropped to her knees, patting at one of the chairs and then the surrounding floor. Elizabeth, holding the second lantern, checked the second chair and the carpeting beneath.

"It is not here," Lydia said, her voice tightening. "What if I lost it while we were sailing? It could be on the boat, and if there's rain and wind, it will wash away."

This is why Elizabeth had told Lydia not to wear the jewelry for their sailing excursion, not that Lydia had listened. Elizabeth said, "Do you remember when you last had it?"

"Yes. It was there when we were dining on the ship, for certain. I touched it as Mr. Dunham was flirting with Miss Bingley. So romantic! He has eyes for no other."

Elizabeth said, "Perhaps Mr. Whitmore or Mr. Stanton found it on the boat after we left? We can ask them in the morning."

"But if they did not, then— It is but a short walk. Let us just look."

Elizabeth glanced at the time, half ten. "We cannot pay call to Mr. Dunham at half 10. It will be near eleven before we arrived and roused the house."

"We do not have to rouse the house. We can climb onto the boat and look around."

"Absolutely not! They will assume we are thieves, or worse."

"Then you rouse the house, and I will search the boat. That way they will know we are not thieves."

"I will not participate in this."

"Then I shall ask Mrs. Forster and you can stay here and criticize, as you always do."

Elizabeth clenched the lantern as a hot coal of rage burned in her chest. "You call me critical? I have tried to protect you. I am only here because father insisted I come to ensure your virtue."

Lydia breathed in sharply and wiped her fist under her eye. "Papa has always loved you best. Even more so than Jane—and everybody loves Jane. It is not fair!"

No, it was not fair.

Lydia said, "I do not wish your help further. I will find it on my own."

Elizabeth took a step toward her sister. "I do not mean to hurt you."

"Just go."

Elizabeth, though part of her cried to stay, familial loyalty could not outweigh Lydia's dismissal of Elizabeth's efforts to help. Elizabeth had even wrestled the blasted seal. She said, "If you do not see it here, we will call on Mr. Dunham in the morning. It is likely Mr. Whitmore or Mr. Stanton found it on the deck, if it is to be found."

Lydia nodded but did not meet Elizabeth's eyes.

Elizabeth took the second lantern and returned to their shared room. She laid the novel in her lap and attempted to read. The words blurred in front of her eyes. She had wished to help Jane and failed. She had wished to help Lydia, and Lydia was no better off for Elizabeth's presence than if Elizabeth had stayed home. This seaside visit grew worse and worse with each passing moment.

Elizabeth hoped Lydia did not indulge in more sherry and tears. She glanced at the clock, fifteen minutes. Lydia would return soon. Perhaps it would be best if Elizabeth blew out the lantern and went to bed. She could, at the least, get out of her afternoon clothes. Her stays were constricting and her bodice itched.

Elizabeth took out the letter she had written to Jane, unfolded it, and read through it again. She would send this letter and the one she had written upon discovering Mr. Bingley here, to Jane. Jane would forgive her. Jane forgave everyone. The question was if Elizabeth deserved Jane's forgiveness.

Another ten minutes passed.

Where was Lydia? It should not take so long to search one room. Perhaps she had taken more of the sherry and now lay in a drunken sleep in Mrs. Forster's parlor.

If so, it was Elizabeth's responsibility to wake her and drag her to bed. Hopefully the morning's headache would be enough to convince Lydia why it was best not to overindulge.

Elizabeth went back down the stairs to the parlor. The room was dark. "Lydia?"

Silence.

Elizabeth held her lantern out and looked first

at the chairs for Lydia, eyes shut, legs sprawled over the arm of one. But the chairs were empty, as was the piano bench and the floor.

Elizabeth's heart pounded. Dratted Lydia. She could not have left the house without attracting notice, could she?

Hoping against an instinct which led Elizabeth, from experience, to expect the absolute worst of her sister, she went to Mrs. Forster's room. Maybe Lydia found the earring and had gone to Mrs. Forster to lament Elizabeth's cruelty.

That was most likely. Lydia would not have left Mrs. Forester's home and snuck off to Mr. Dunham's to search his boat in the middle of the night. Even Lydia could not be so foolish.

Elizabeth climbed the stairs again, passing her own room and continuing down the hall to Mrs. Forster's.

Elizabeth knocked.

Silence.

"Mrs. Forster?"

Nothing. Elizabeth knocked louder. At her third attempt, the door opened. Mrs. Forster, in her nightrail, stared blearily at Elizabeth.

"I am sorry to wake you, but have you seen Lydia?"

"We were in the parlor earlier. Have you checked there?"

Elizabeth explained about the earring and Lydia's disappearance.

"You think she went on her own?"

"I do not know. I cannot imagine Lydia would be so foolish."

Mrs. Forster bit her bottom lip. "Have you checked the kitchens? Lydia is likely hiding from you. She—" Miss Forster rubbed her eyes. "Have you considered treating her with more kindness?"

Elizabeth clenched her hand around the lantern handle. More kindness? Elizabeth had been nothing but kind. Her temper sometimes got the better of her, but that was only to be expected, considering Lydia's appalling behavior most of the time.

But perhaps Mrs. Forster was right that Lydia would enjoy giving Elizabeth a scare, especially if she felt Elizabeth was being unreasonable. Lydia was in no shape for wandering at night.

Mrs. Forster said, "I can dress and help you search, if you would like."

Elizabeth shook her head. "I have inconvenienced you enough. You know her better than I do, I fear. I will check the kitchens and the other rooms."

"Or you can go to bed. Lydia is certain to return in the morning."

Elizabeth thanked Mrs. Forster again and stepped away from her room. Mrs. Forster shut the door with a quiet click.

Elizabeth wanted to believe Mrs. Forster. But a horrible sense of dread, the same sense that had overtaken Elizabeth when Lydia cheerfully took her hand and dragged her into the seaside shack hiding a gambling hell, packed with young, hungry men, grew stronger.

Lydia was sauced and angry. As much as it compounded the problem for Elizabeth to follow on her own, without even Mrs. Forster to provide the veneer of a chaperone, Elizabeth could not wait. Every minute that passed put Lydia in further danger. Elizabeth could count on her quick wits and sobriety. Lydia had neither.

Elizabeth found a shawl to wrap over her clothing. She pulled her hair back in a simple knot, hoping to be mistaken at a distance as a servant. The shawl at least was a dark gray.

Elizabeth's mouth was dry and her hands sweating on the handle of a lantern when she stepped outside. The wind had picked up, and though the moon, three-quarters full, and a patch of stars was visible ahead, towards the sea, clouds gathered like thick, dirty wool.

Elizabeth's habit of taking long walks had given her an excellent sense of direction. She remembered the route the carriage had taken and followed it in reverse.

She hoped Lydia, in her drunken state, had wandered in the correct direction. It would triple this foolishness if Lydia had, intending to search Mr. Dunham's boat, gone off in a different direction and found trouble without Elizabeth's dubious attempt at rescue.

Elizabeth put the shawl over her head, wrapping one edge over her bodice. With the fabric of the shawl obscuring her face, she would be less recognizable.

Elizabeth shuttered the lantern, hoping the clouds stayed at sea long enough for her to make it to and from Mr. Dunham's house. She doubted it. Lightening flashed. As Elizabeth walked, the air felt thick with the promise of a storm.

What if Lydia had fallen and harmed herself? What if brigands or other unsavory types had captured her? What if—?

With each step, Elizabeth grew more afraid. Not for herself. Though Elizabeth had put herself in the same danger as her sister, she refused to doubt her own abilities.

Perhaps she and Lydia were not so different.

Clouds moved in, covering the moon. Lightning purpled the clouds above, and a few seconds later, thunder rumbled.

Two young gentlemen, one with his arm thrown over the other's shoulders, both singing loudly, turned towards her from the opposite side of the street. Elizabeth slipped into the shadow of the closest building, hid the lantern with her body, and froze.

The young men, caught in their own revelry, continued on without paying her the slightest mind.

Elizabeth shivered and clutched her shawl. What was she doing? What if Lydia was hiding somewhere in the house? Then Elizabeth was putting herself and all of her sisters in grave peril by wandering alone to Brighton at night.

But if Lydia had gone, then Elizabeth owed it to her sister to follow. Lydia might be silly, selfish and, at times, a brat, but she was Elizabeth's sister. Elizabeth loved Lydia anyway. Was that not the core of love, seeing the good despite another's faults?

Elizabeth thought again of Mr. Darcy and Mr. Bingley. Mr. Darcy, in his ill-tempered proposal, had outlined all of Elizabeth's faults and declared his love. Mr. Bingley, in contrast, seemed enamored of Jane's virtues, but at the slightest hint of a fault, one he had not even observed, he had fled, cut ties, and broken Jane's heart.

Which was the better man?

A drop of rain touched her face. In the distance, thunder rumbled. If Lydia had come out in this, she would return to the house before getting caught in a storm. Even as a child, Lydia had hated mud.

Elizabeth took a calming breath and walked again.

But when she arrived at Mr. Dunham's dock, three large men in dark clothes were on the boat, their movements angry shadows, while, on the dock, Mr. Dunham stood, speaking with a third man. He had a wide face and scarred nose that looked like the beak of a bird of prey.

Elizabeth was too far away to make out more than their form, and they moved quietly, communicating with hand signals. She shrank back.

If Lydia was on that ship...no—! She couldn't be.

On the sailboat's deck, one of the men knelt at the base of the largest sail. He pulled at something, a struggling form.

"Help!"

Elizabeth's stomach churned as she recognized the voice.

Lydia, the blasted, dratted fool!

Thunder rumbled, and six seconds later, lightning lit the sky, causing the clouds to glow.

The man pulled Lydia upright and grabbed her, smothering her face against his shoulder. Lydia struggled.

Elizabeth, leaped up, or tried to, but someone grabbed her from behind. Thunder clapped again, muffling Elizabeth's scream as the man put his hand over her mouth. He whispered, "Quiet!"

# CHAPTER 19

D arcy cradled a glass of port and paced three steps forward and three steps back, while Bingley put the bottle back in his traveling chest.

"Darcy, please. Just tell me what it is before you walk a hole in the carpeting."

"I proposed to Miss Elizabeth." Best to say it plainly. "At Rosings. She was visiting Mrs. Collins, and my cousin and I paid call on my aunt."

"I remember you mentioned to visit, but Miss Elizabeth was there? And..." Bingley took a swallow of his port. "You should have had us order whiskey."

"I thought myself in love."

Bingley raised his eyebrows. "Miss Elizabeth was open to your regard?"

Darcy took a sip of his port. Mortifying as this was, sharing his failed proposal was the easier part of this confession. "I had thought so. I was mistaken."

Bingley sighed. "I am surprised you would risk your heart with the second Bennet knowing the character of the first." He drank again. "Love makes fools of us all. Though if it is as you said, and the Bennet sisters were interested only in wealth, Miss Elizabeth ought to have seized the chance to become Lady of Pemberley."

Darcy rubbed his fingers on his temple. "Miss Elizabeth— I should have spoken earlier, but I had not the opportunity to confirm what she told me."

"What did she tell you?"

"Miss Bennet. Miss Jane Bennet, she was, perhaps, as enamored of you as you of her. In Netherfield."

Bingley jumped to his feet. "Miss Elizabeth told you Miss Jane was fond of me?"

Miserably, Darcy nodded.

"But you visited Rosings months ago. How is it only now you share this with me? I thought we were friends." Bingley finished his glass in one long swallow and, hand still gripping the glass, said, "Explain yourself."

"Miss Elizabeth made clear I was the last man she would marry, and when I revealed to her my advice to you, she was further hardened in her perspective. But you must understand, Miss Elizabeth is not a fair judge of character, though she may think herself such. She thought Wickham honorable and wronged by me and—"

"Mr. Wickham was a stranger to her, but her sister, it is clear how close they are, and yet you doubted her?"

"I intended to rectify my error."

"It has been months, Darcy."

"And if her affection has changed, what good would I have done to further exacerbate your loss? You are my friend, and I had no wish to hurt you."

"I am a man, Darcy, not a child." Bingley shook his head. "I cannot speak with you now. Just go."

"I will pack my things. But about Mr. Dunham and your sister—"

"You see the worst of all people. At first, I thought your sharp judgment something admirable, but now… Perhaps it is only you wish everyone to be as miserable and lonely as yourself."

Bingley's words were a hand squeezing Darcy's

lungs. He could not breathe. It was as bad as Elizabeth's rejection. Worse. He and Bingley had been friends since childhood. Now, that friendship was over.

Perhaps Bingley was right. Darcy ruined everything he touched. Had he been more understanding of Georgiana, he might have learned of her relationship with Wickham before his attempted seduction. If Darcy had been more open to Miss Jane Bennet, who had displayed her affection for Bingley in a way he understood even as Darcy did not, then Bingley would have love, and perhaps Darcy would not have ruined his chances with Miss Elizabeth.

Darcy nodded." I am sorry."

Bingley gave no acknowledgment of Darcy's words.

Yes, Darcy had made a hash of things. He left Bingley's room, shutting the door behind him.

Darcy returned to his hotel room, and, waking his valet, informed him to pack Darcy's things as they would leave in the morning.

"What has happened?"

"I cannot—" Darcy could not speak of it, nor could he stay in this room. He still held the half-empty glass of port. Darcy finished it.

Bingley was right, it should have been whiskey.

But there was not enough whiskey in the world to blind him to his mistakes.

Darcy said, "I will return." He would walk. If fortune smiled, he might find an opportunity to exercise the boxing skills Richard had taught him. Not that Darcy expected to win. He would relish getting in a few blows before his opponent beat pain into his flesh, enough, hopefully, to distract Darcy from the pain in his heart at losing his closest friend.

Darcy placed the empty glass on his nightstand and left. He avoided the New Steyne with its outdoor performances and wealthy ladies and gentlemen hoping to catch each other's eyes. Darcy had no interest in fashion or impressing others. And happy conversation would only make it sharper how alone Darcy was.

Darcy walked without intent, but a part of him, having nothing else to fix, wondered at the crates Mr. Dunham had 'won'. Why had no servants been called to take them into his home? Mr. Dunham ought to have wished the wine stored in his cellars. And how had he been so fortunate to win six great cases of wine and to happen upon the captain in such a coincidental manner?

Bingley, inclined towards generosity, would over-look this, but even as Darcy's suspicious nature had failed him time and again, he could not deny the certainty that Dunham was involved in something more than a friendly sailors' bet.

Thunder rumbled, and lightening lit the clouds above, but when Darcy arrived in sight of Dunham's home, the gentleman was outside, standing on his dock. He glanced at his pocket watch, which glinted in the lantern's light on the ground beside him.

Whom was he waiting for? If Darcy had been inclined to act the proper gentleman, he would have called out and spoken with Dunham. But Darcy suspected the man was up to no good, so he hid himself and waited.

A man wearing fisherman's clothes arrived. He was older, his face weathered, his nose a scarred beak. He and Mr. Dunham conversed, and a moment later, the man waved three others forward who, at Mr. Dunham's direction, climbed onto the boat.

Darcy saw a small figure in light blue run across the deck and hide beneath one of the sails.

Dunham and the older man spoke, perhaps negotiating. Darcy considered slipping away to ask someone in a neighboring house to call for a constable, but then he saw a woman walking towards them.

Though the shawl obscured her forehead, Darcy could not mistake her face. Miss Elizabeth! Had he not warned her? What was she doing here, in the middle of the night, alone?

Miss Elizabeth at least had the sense not to call out to Mr. Dunham, rousing the others and putting her in greater peril. Darcy did not know what business Mr. Dunham had with these men, though he suspected it had something to do with the crates, which he now was certain did not contain Spanish wine. He crept from his hiding spot towards Miss Elizabeth, who, in a stroke of rare good fortune, seemed to have spotted an alcove and was now sneaking towards it.

"Help!" A young woman screamed from the boat.

Elizabeth moved, and Darcy, recognizing the danger she was in, grabbed her, putting his hand over her mouth and whispering her to be quiet.

Elizabeth struggled.

"It is me. Darcy. Please," he whispered again.

Elizabeth froze.

Thankfully, the men were too occupied with the events on the boat to notice Darcy and Elizabeth.

One of the smugglers dragged a young, fair-haired woman from her hiding place. Her head pressed into his shoulder, muffling her screams.

Elizabeth whimpered.

Rain touched Darcy's face. It was only a few drops, but lightning flashed again, and Darcy's hair trembled in the growing wind.

The large man said something to her, and the young woman went still.

The older man, who Dunham had been speaking with, demanded, "What is this?"

Dunham shook his head. "I do not know! I want this as much as you do. You must believe it."

The man loosened his grip and allowed the young woman to turn. "Do you know this mite?" he asked.

Miss Lydia. It all made sense now. Miss Elizabeth's sister had run off, and she had followed. But why had she done so alone?

"Mr. Dunham!" Lydia shouted. "I lost my earring. Do you see?" Lydia held up something in her fingers.

Miss Elizabeth muttered something under her breath.

Lydia said, "I did not mean to interrupt your… meeting? I have my earring. I will leave now."

"We cannot let her go," the man on the dock said.

"Miss Lydia knows nothing. She is just a child."

Miss Elizabeth whispered, "Mr. Darcy, they're going to—hurt her." She swallowed, shaking in his arms.

Darcy said, "They will not." How Darcy would ensure such a thing, he had no idea, but he would.

Dunham said, "Let her go. I will smooth things over with your employer and—"

"Your fine hands are not made for gutting fish," the older man said. "The girl will come with us."

Mr. Dunham, to his credit, said, "I cannot allow this."

"Then, when our business is complete, take her with you and dispose of her yourself."

Another flash of lightning, then thunder, and the rain fell harder, beating heavy drops against the dock and ground.

The man holding Miss Lydia walked her to the chest where they had stored their dinner earlier that afternoon and forced her to sit. He waved to one of the other men, who went to the rigging and pulled out a length of rope.

Rain hit Darcy's face. He wiped his hand over his forehead, blinking it from his lashes.

The other men resumed carrying up crates from below and passing them man to man to rest on the dock.

The older man said, "Since you want to bring the girl along, you will have to pull your weight." He gestured to the crates stacked on the dock.

Dunham knelt and lifted the crate. He strained beneath its weight.

Darcy was not familiar with smuggling practices, but he recognized a trap when he saw one. With Dunham focused on carrying the heavy crates of goods, he would be too tired to question the men and what they were doing with Lydia. Now that he expected Mr. Dunham to help. Dunham was in this up to his neck, Miss Lydia an unfortunate bystander.

Darcy whispered to Elizabeth, "Get a Constable." He let her go. "Go to the nearest neighbor." Help would not arrive in time, but at least Miss Elizabeth would not have to witness any harm to her sister.

"I cannot leave her," Miss Elizabeth said.

Lydia shrank back, turning her body away from the men. Her feet moved. Was she kicking off her shoes? The second man walked over, and when he was close enough, tossed the length of rope to the first.

Barefoot, Lydia ran. The men grabbed for her, but Miss Lydia was too fast, her skirts flaring behind her as she ran, not towards the dock as Darcy expected, but to the boat's stern.

One of the other men caught hold of her dress, but Lydia's speed was such his grip tore away a section of the fabric. Lydia, in a desperate leap, threw herself into the sea.

## CHAPTER 20

Lydia was an excellent swimmer, but the weight of her clothes would drag her down, in spite of her own strength in the water. Elizabeth jumped up, heedless of the men or her own danger. Lydia needed help, and Elizabeth was there to keep her sister safe. Elizabeth futilely tore at the bindings on her dress as she ran to the water, the rain-slick wood of the dock causing her to stumble and nearly fall before she reached the edge.

One of the smugglers cursed as another yelled.

Darcy called out, "Constable! What is the meaning of this?"

Mr. Dunham dropped his crate, jumped back and shouted, "Stop! Thief!"

*Cad!* Darcy thought.

But it rattled the smugglers.

Their leader called out, "On the wagon! Go!"

Though they only had three of the crates loaded, the others dropped the rest of their ill-gotten goods and ran.

Their leader jumped onto the wagon and, climbing into the driver's seat, whipped the horses. The others dashed for the wagon, and one made it, throwing himself on the back and rolling. The others, too late, split up and ran.

Elizabeth at the least had shed her dress. Wearing only a thin undergarment, she kicked free her boots and jumped into the frigid water.

The cold knocked the breath out of her as the rain, heavier now, pocked the water. Thunder rumbled, and a few seconds later, the sky glowed again.

Elizabeth spotted Lydia and swam to her sister, who gasped, splashing.

Though loosened, the stays still weighted her down, and Elizabeth felt like she was dragging a weight as she struggled to reach her sister.

The chill water further sapped her strength.

Lydia's head went under.

Elizabeth's guts turned to ice. A moment later,

Lydia's head surfaced. Thunder rumbled a third time, and the rain came down hard and fast, blurring Elizabeth's vision as she swam.

"Lydia!"

"Lizz—"

The lightning showed her sister slipping below the water again.

Elizabeth kicked. She was close enough to reach out, and she did, grasping her sister's hand as it sank below the rain pocked water.

Elizabeth sucked in a breath and went under, gripping her sister's hand and pulling with all of her strength. But Lydia was too heavy, and they were both going down.

Elizabeth's lungs burned. She tried to pull again, but hers and her sister's clothes were too heavy.

Something, or someone, slipped under her arm.

It was one of the brigands, Elizabeth's only hope for their help. She could not see. Her eyes were squeezed shut in the water and even if they were not, it was too dark.

Elizabeth's chest burned. Her fingers, which had ached upon hitting the chilly water, now numbed even as she desperately struggled to maintain her grip of her sister's hand.

Elizabeth kicked, desperate to bring herself and her sister to the surface. She was faint, her lungs contracting.

Cold. So cold. The thunder and rain were gone. She floated in a sea of cold. Had she lost her grip?

Something wrenched her sister away.

Elizabeth kicked again, and it was easier now.

Whoever it was, was helping. If it was a brigand, Elizabeth was still grateful to him.

Elizabeth broke the surface and gasped. Rain fell down her face. The thunder mingled with her heartbeat. Darcy was beside her, close enough to touch except Elizabeth's hands gripped Lydia's wrist and she could not unbend them.

Lydia was limp, eyes shut, and Mr. Darcy held her, one arm beneath hers, his hands clasped around her chest, holding her head above the water. Something splashed into the water beside them. A leather-clad plank of wood, attached to a rope. Elizabeth recognized it as one of the bumpers Mr. Dunham had deployed when meeting with the *Lucia Itzel*.

From the deck, Mr. Dunham shouted, take it, I'll pull you in!" a second bumper splashed into the water, on Elizabeth's right.

Elizabeth grabbed the second, while Mr. Darcy,

holding Lydia in one arm now, took the float with his other.

Elizabeth reached the wood and hung on. She was too tired to manage anything further. The wood was buoyant, and Elizabeth pressed her face to the leather as the rain washed over her.

Lydia coughed, and something inside Elizabeth lightened. Lydia was alive!

Darcy said, "Miss Lydia, you are safe."

Though Mr. Darcy spoke to Lydia, Elizabeth felt the warmth of his words. Her heart clung to Mr. Darcy's words as the storm raged.

# CHAPTER 21

Darcy's heart stopped as Elizabeth threw herself in the water. Surely she did not mean to end her life! Darcy ran after, kicking off his shoes and shedding his clothes as he ran. In the water, Miss Lydia struggled to stay afloat as Miss Elizabeth swam towards her. But no matter the strength of their swimming, the water was cold and they were weighed down by heavy frocks.

Darcy, stripped down to his trousers and socks, dove into the water.

Lydia slipped under, a few seconds later surfacing for a moment before dropping again. Miss Elizabeth swam towards her as Darcy swam towards them both. In his trousers, his strong, lanky form could sweep through the water with greater speed. Within eight strokes, he reached Miss Elizabeth. She went under.

Heart pounding, Darcy took a breath and kicked down, reaching frantically for her. As Darcy reached out, he recognized Miss Elizabeth's tight grip on her sister's arm. She would not let go.

To rescue Elizabeth, he would have to rescue Miss Lydia. Darcy swam beneath Miss Lydia and, grabbing her about the waist, kicked upwards.

Miss Elizabeth, at least recognizing that Miss Lydia was being carried upwards, kicked to the surface. With Darcy's help, the two young ladies were above water again, at least for now. But there was still the matter of bringing them to shore. Darcy was strong, but he doubted he could drag two waterlogged young ladies to shore on his own. Not without some help.

Something hit the water with a splash. Darcy, heart pounding, looked for one of the smugglers.

No smuggler. Instead, a piece of wood with rope attached to it. A second one hit the water, and Miss Elizabeth splashed towards it. Darcy, dragging Miss Lydia, who was far too still, grabbed at the other leather-clad plank, which, as he caught his breath, he realized must have been from Mr. Dunham's boat.

"He held Lydia above the surface, and, to his relief, she started to cough.

Mr. Dunham, running with the two opposite ends of the long rope, leapt off of the sailboat and onto the dock. Darcy, exhausted, clung to the plank. As Dunham pulled them in. Miss Lydia whipped her elbow back, kicking her feet.

"Stop," Darcy said. "They are gone. You are safe.

"Mr. Darcy?" Miss Lydia coughed again.

"You are safe," Darcy repeated.

Despite the storm raging, Miss Lydia relaxed in his arms.

When they reached the dock, Miss Elizabeth called out to Mr. Dunham to bring in Mr. Darcy and Lydia first.

Darcy's chest ached with a mix of pride and lingering terror. How could Miss Elizabeth have been so foolish? But he knew. Darcy would have done the same for anyone he loved.

Love.

The word was as bitter as the salt on his lips and as stinging as the salt in his eyes.

When Darcy reached the edge of the dock, he pushed Miss Lydia to Mr. Dunham, who knelt over the side of the dock and grabbed her by the arms. Darcy, in the water, could do little to help lift Lydia up, but Mr. Dunham managed. When Miss Lydia was coughing on the dock, Dunham leaned down with his arm to Darcy, who said, "Get Miss Elizabeth." He would not bear the thought of losing her again. Not for a third time. That moment she had hit the water, Darcy's entire world stopped.

As Mr. Dunham pulled Miss Elizabeth next onto the dock, Darcy clung to the wood, the chill of the water numbing his skin and quelling the fire of his fear and rage. Mr. Dunham leaned over, extending an arm, and Darcy took it. Mr. Dunham heaved him up, and Darcy knelt, wet and shivering on the dock.

The rain had eased some, instead of falling in sheets, it now beat fat drops against the dock's wooden planks.

Miss Elizabeth clung to her sister, who sobbed, "Lizzy, I am so sorry. I never— You warned me, and I did not listen. I am so sorry."

"No matter," Elizabeth said, stroking her sister's hair. She was crying too.

Mr. Dunham said, "You must understand, I meant no one to be hurt. Those men— It is... Miss Caroline will never— I had thought, what is the harm in helping to bring French Brandy across the channel? We all drink it in the clubs."

Darcy said, "Was it Mr. Wickham who put you in contact with these men?"

"Yes. He is involved with other things too, I am certain. Mr. Wickham's work in records allows him knowledge of where militia and, somehow, naval patrols, will be stationed. I do not know the extent of his network. Though Wickham himself has no true power beyond the information. Please, do not tell Miss Bingley of my shame. I will leave, and never return, please do not tell her. My father's mistakes will soon be known to all."

"Will you tell the constable and militia commander what you know of this operation?"

"I will tell them everything. I had never meant to hurt anyone. With the money, I wanted to give Miss Bingley the life she deserves. It hardly matters now, but I have grown very fond of Miss Bingley. Not that she would ever pay mind to a man without fortune. She will find a man worthy of her. It was foolish to believe that might be me."

Miss Elizabeth said, "Why not leave that to her discretion?"

Darcy froze. Miss Elizabeth was defending Mr. Dunham?

Mr. Dunham said, "I cannot ask that of her. She will believe I am only marrying her for her dowry."

Darcy said, "You cannot stay in Brighton. Once these men discover you have turned on them, they will not be pleased."

Mr. Dunham nodded. "I shall return to London. My father suggested we make our way in the colonies, and I suppose with the sale of the *Artemis*, we shall have enough to fund the voyage and—" He swallowed. "That is what I should've done. Now, I am twice cursed."

Miss Elizabeth said, "If you had not saved us, we would have drowned, and no one would know your crimes. But you saved us. The others ran, and you stayed. That must be worth something."

Darcy recognized the truth in Elizabeth's words. Mr. Dunham had saved them. When Miss Elizabeth had gone into the water, Darcy knew he would've given his life to save hers, and without Dunham's help, he would have given his life and hers for nothing. There was a debt between them.

Worse, Darcy could not share the full accounting of this evening without damaging Miss Elizabeth's and Miss Lydia's virtue. If anyone discovered the events of this evening, both young ladies would be forever compromised.

"You will leave Miss Bingley be," Darcy said.

"It is worse if you leave without a word," Elizabeth said, more forcefully. "Write a letter, at the least."

"I cannot. It would be improper."

"Sometimes the most improper thing is the correct one," Elizabeth said. Her dark eyes met his, and Darcy realized this was a test. One, this time, he would not fail.

"Write her," Darcy said. "I will take it from my hands to hers. You have my word."

Mr. Dunham nodded. "My home is an embarrassment," he said. "I have had to sell some things. But I suppose that does not matter now. I will get blankets and Stanton will have the carriage readied."

"Mr. Stanton?" Lydia asked.

"I am not adept at sailing." Mr. Dunham said with a sigh. "And now, I suppose I have no more secrets."

"None but this," Darcy said, glancing at the two young Bennet ladies. "We will speak no more of tonight."

Mr. Dunham nodded. "Thank you, Mr. Darcy. You cannot know—"

"I know," Darcy said.

"Blankets. And the carriage." Mr. Dunham bowed and jogged to his house.

When the carriage was readied, Darcy went to Miss Elizabeth. "You are well?"

Elizabeth turned her luminous dark eyes to his. "You saved us," she said.

"I could not let you fall."

Miss Elizabeth swallowed. "Thank you," she said.

Darcy took her hand. Though Mr. Dunham had given each girl a thick duvet, Miss Elizabeth's fingers were still icy to the touch. He squeezed her bare hand. "When you jumped, it almost ended me."

Elizabeth swallowed, and her lashes glittered with tears. "I felt you beside me, in the water. And later, what you said to Lydia, you also said it to me."

"I should like to call on you, tomorrow, if you will allow it. Before I leave."

"You cannot leave." Elizabeth gripped his hand. "I will not let you."

Darcy wanted to take Miss Elizabeth in his arms and kiss her until they both, once again, strained to breathe. But she was distraught, and he would not take advantage. It was enough that she lived, and they would see each other again in a few hours.

Elizabeth stood up on her tiptoes, and, still gripping his hand, whispered, "Tomorrow."

Darcy nodded. The hardest thing was opening his hands to let her go.

The rest of the evening was far less pleasant. Darcy and Dunham agreed to a story that would protect the young ladies' reputation and to some extent Mr. Dunham's. They called for the constable, and Mr. Dunham explained how his boat had been robbed and vandalized, describing the wagon and the three men. He said, "I believe they were acquaintances of Mr. Wickham. We met over a game of cards."

It was past three in the morning when Darcy returned to the hotel.

He changed from his salt-damp clothes and asked his valet to wake him the next morning at nine.

"Are you to follow Mr. Bingley then?"

"Follow him where?"

Darcy's valet shrugged. "There's talk Mr. Bingley made for the nearest Posting Inn to return to Netherfield. He would not wait until morning, hoping to shave some hours from his journey."

"So Bingley meant to mend fences with Miss Bennet. Darcy hoped she still had feelings for his friend. Though Bingley might never forgive him, Darcy wished Bingley happy.

With that thought, Darcy fell onto the blankets and closed his eyes, opening them what felt like mere seconds later to a shake on his shoulder.

Limbs heavy and eyes gummed with sleep, he yawned and sat up. He had given his word to Miss Elizabeth and would not break it.

Darcy called for breakfast to his room, and, unpacking his finest morning suit, dressed. Even as he did so, he berated himself for foolishness. Miss Elizabeth had already declared him the last man she wished to marry. The previous evening, she had been understandably distraught. She had gripped him reaching for safety, not as an invitation to romance. Both she and he would be better off if he left. But he had given his word, and he could not bear the thought of leaving Brighton without seeing her again.

Darcy could not bear the thought of another string of days without her laugh, her observations, or the way she challenged him. He wished to know if she fit as well in his arms as he imagined she would. No, he would not leave. He would speak with her and discover if there was any chance.

Perhaps, she might be more open to his proposal a second time.

Proposing a second time, it was unheard of. And yet...

Darcy had no answers. Only hope.

Standing on the front step of the Forster's Brighton home, Darcy doubted himself again. He ought at least have brought flowers. No. Flowers were too forward.

The door opened, and a footman said, "Mr. Darcy? Mr. Fitzwilliam Darcy?"

Darcy nodded.

"This way."

# CHAPTER 22

Outside, thunder rumbled. Bingley knew himself a fool to leave in the middle of the night for the Posting Inn with only a small chest of clothes. What purpose did it serve to shave mere hours from a journey months past due? He was furious at Darcy for keeping Miss Jane's affection from him. Blast Darcy's interfering nature! Blast Darcy and his inability to trust anyone but himself!

Bingley was through being the amiable companion to a suspicious lout.

If only Bingley had trusted his own heart, he and Miss Bennet might already be married.

Though Bingley had insisted they make haste, the driver spurred the horses to a measured trot, fearing they might lose a shoe or misstep and injure themselves. Bingley understood, though the caution frustrated him. Mostly he cursed himself. His heart had known Miss Jane Bennet's character, but he had listened to doubts and fled.

Heavy drops of rain hit the roof of the carriage. They had been riding twenty minutes. And the Posting Inn was ten minutes further still, at the edge of Brighton. They should arrive soon. Then, Bingley could take a room and sleep in discomfort and wake at first light to continue his trek. The rain would make going treacherous.

Bingley cursed himself again.

When they arrived at the Posting Inn, the driver and horses were drenched. Thankfully, there were still rooms available. Bingley had not the foresight to check ahead. His horses were stabled, and he ordered the smallest, lightest carriage they had to rent and a change of horses every few hours to speed his journey to Netherfield.

Though dubious of the weather allowing Bingley to leave at first light as he had planned, the innkeeper agreed to Bingley's terms and happily accepted payment. Bingley spent a fitful night on a narrow, uncomfortable bed and arose to a milky dawn. Reluctantly, he agreed to wait until the morning sun had dried out the roads, not wishing to further slow his journey by risking his horses or carriage.

Perhaps he could send a letter ahead, informing Jane of his arrival? Bingley sat in the common room and penned the letter. He then made a show of reading a paper though he was not much for reading. He must have dozed off because in his dreams Miss Bennet called out, "Mr. Bingley?"

Bingley opened his eyes. Miss Jane Bennet was a vision, her blonde curls mussed and her clothing travel-creased, but her face was sweet and her smile made Bingley's heart flutter in his chest. He said, "I must be dreaming. I am to Netherfield to see you and hope you will accept my apology."

Though it was forward, Bingley held out his hand, and to prove he was dreaming, Miss Bennet took it.

Miss Bennet said, "What have you to apologize for?" There was a hint of reproach in her tone, as though she knew his faults and wanted him to acknowledge them to her.

Bingley said, "I was the greatest of fools. I listened to others instead of my heart, and their fears became my own. But if you will have me, fool as I am, I will every day prove to you the truth of my love."

Miss Bennet's eyes shone, she blinked and wiped her knuckles beneath her eyes, smearing tears. Bingley reached in his pocket for his handkerchief and handed it to her.

"Yes" Miss Bennet said, taking the handkerchief. "Yes! I wanted you to tell me, face-to-face, you no longer loved me. My love for you was a great and painful weight I could not shed. Now, to hear these words, to know that our love for each other is true and will be unending, there is no greater happiness."

Bingley rubbed his eyes.

"Miss Bennet?"

"Yes." She took his hands. They were in the public area of the busy Posting Inn, but she took both of his hands and squeezed them. She wore gloves, but he felt the heat of her.

"Tell me I am not dreaming," Bingley said.

"I am uncertain that I am awake either, Mr. Bingley." Miss Bennet's cheeks colored.

"If I am awake, tell me again you accept my proposal of marriage," Bingley said.

"I accept. And if I awake, then come with me to

Brighton so you may tell my sisters of our happiness."

"We shall go, together."

Bingley stood. Heedless of the onlookers, who waited in the public room, as he had, for the roads to improve, Bingley pulled Jane close.

Miss Bennet, no, Jane, his Jane, lifted her chin, and they kissed. The heat of her lips and the scent of honeysuckle finally convinced Bingley that this was not, as he feared, a dream, but the start of something beautiful.

Not the start. The continuation.

In the carriage, together with Jane's chaperone, an older maid in Mrs. Gardiner's employ who had the noteworthy aspect of being both hard of hearing and focused on her correspondence, Jane asked, "What brought you back to me?"

"Darcy." Bingley sighed. "He turned me from you and turned me back, after a discussion with your sister."

"I am certain she gave him an earful."

Bingley, his fury eased by his current joy, smiled. "She broke his heart, so I suppose that makes us even."

"There is no joy in that kind of fairness," Jane said.

Bingley sighed. "I will forgive him. After he stews a bit." He squeezed her hand and leaned closer, breathing in her sweetness. "Now that I no longer doubt my judgment, I will say, if they can get past themselves, they might be well suited."

Jane giggled. "Some things are fortunate coincidences, Charles, and others require miracles."

## CHAPTER 23

Elizabeth's heart clung to the memory of Mr. Darcy's hands all the way back to Mrs. Forster's.

Rain beat against the top of Mr. Dunham's carriage as they returned to Mrs. Forster's. Lydia sat curled to Elizabeth's side like a small child. She said, "You jumped in after me."

"You are my sister!"

"I am sorry."

"There is a reason mother tells us not to drink in excess."

"I flirted with Mr. Wickham. It was to make you mad."

"Why?"

Lydia rubbed her thumb along her index finger.

295

"You are so clever and everybody likes you. I've always thought if I could capture a handsome gentleman's attention, it would—make everyone think as well of me as they do of you."

Elizabeth pulled her sister close and said, "I thought you silly too. And foolish. But I was wrong. Because I believed you were only these things, I allowed you no room to be anything else. You are brave. You care for others. And it was clever to jump off the boat, knowing you can swim. Though if you do that again, I will never forgive you."

Lydia giggled.

Normally, Elizabeth found the sound irritating, but now, she was glad to hear it.

Lydia said, "I know we will never be as close as you and Jane, or me and Kitty, to be truthful. But I am glad to have you as my sister, Lizzy."

"And I am glad to have you as mine," Elizabeth said. Yes, Lydia had caused Elizabeth no end of trouble, but Elizabeth wanted the best for her. She hoped this evening's experience taught her caution.

"Good," Lydia said. "Now, you must tell me how you and Mr. Darcy have fallen in love."

"Fallen in love?"

"I know when you answer with a question it is because you don't wish to talk to the subject. We are sisters, so you must tell me everything. As you would Jane. Otherwise I shall never forgive you, and who knows what trouble I will find myself in if I cannot forgive you."

"We are not in love."

"Are you certain?"

Elizabeth pointed at Lydia's bodice. "What is that lump?"

"This?" Lydia smiled, reached into the bodice of her dress and pulled out a single earring.

"You found it!"

"I did. I said I would get it, and I did. Now, if you are forthcoming, I will allow you to wear them and the necklace tomorrow when Mr. Darcy visits.

Elizabeth laughed. "You devilish seal!"

After alighting from the carriage, Elizabeth and Lydia linked arms. Elizabeth did not tell Lydia everything. But she told her enough. And the next morning, Lydia, Mrs. Forster, and Elizabeth drank chocolate and ate eggs and toast while pretending not to wait for their first morning caller.

Mrs. Forster said, "You are fortunate my husband was away for the evening, else—" Mrs. Forster shook her head, repeating herself for about the thirtieth time that morning about their late night excursion. "You cannot do this again,

Lydia. You must take some care with your virtue. I asked you here to introduce you to eligible young men, not for you to be gallivanting in the night like—"

Elizabeth said, "I am certain my sister has learned her lesson."

"And you!" Why did you follow her? I told you to return to your bed."

Elizabeth took a bite of her toast.

A knock sounded at the door, and Elizabeth adjusted her dress. Her mother's necklace lay at her collarbone, and the earrings hung, brushing her neck as she turned her head to the door.

The footman announced, "Mr. Fitzwilliam Darcy."

Mr. Darcy entered and bowed. He was dressed more formally than the morning occasioned, and Elizabeth, who had donned her best afternoon frock in anticipation of his call, stood and curtsied. "Mr. Darcy."

"I hope it is not an inconvenience to call so early."

"No!" Elizabeth cut in before Mrs. Forster or Miss Lydia could speak.

Lydia stood and with a brief curtsy said, "I cannot thank you enough for your help last night,

Mr. Darcy. My sister would have perished without your help."

Of course, Lydia did not acknowledge the dangers she put herself in.

Mr. Darcy said, "It was my pleasure to be of assistance to you both."

"And Mr. Dunham?" Miss Elizabeth asked.

"He shared with a constable how he came upon those men robbing his boat. It was fortunate I was there to assist, and we ran them off.

Though Elizabeth had expected no less of Mr. Darcy, who was more discreet a man than she had suspected before his revelations at Rosings and later in his letter; she was still relieved neither she nor Lydia's reputations would suffer for their excursion.

Mrs. Forster said, "I am certain Mr. Dunham was grateful for your help. You saw nothing else?"

"The storm was fierce, and anything else would have been a trick of the memory or light," Mr. Darcy said.

"I am glad you are well," Elizabeth said. She wished to take a step towards him. She wished to exchange more than simple pleasantries, but how could she show herself open to him after rejecting him so before? He had saved her life. Perhaps he only wished to check on her welfare now? No. She would not let fear stop her from opening her heart. Elizabeth said, "Some judgments, I made earlier, at your aunt's, I feel now were in error."

"I, too, made judgments in error."

Something inside Elizabeth broke. She lowered her head. "I understand."

"No! Not that. I meant, I told Bingley of your sister's—"

"You did?" Elizabeth's mouth was dry.

"He did not take it well. But I believe he will remedy his error. If she is still open to him."

Elizabeth could breathe again." That is... Wonderful!"

Lydia, who had been doing a remarkable job of staying silent, exclaimed, "Mr. Bingley does love Jane! I told her. And Jane should be here within the next day or so, how grand!"

Elizabeth whirled to her sister. "Jane is coming?"

"I wrote Jane the first day, when we saw Mr. Bingley in the carriage."

Jane would not have agreed to travel all the way to Brighton simply for the knowledge Mr. Bingley was here. He had ignored her for an entire month in London. Elizabeth's eyes narrowed, "What else did you tell her?"

"Only that Bingley held affection for her—"

"You had only seen him in the carriage. You lied to our sister!"

"I did not. He holds affection for Jane, and how could he not? Jane is beautiful and has the sweetest disposition." Her voice lowered on the last word, and she shot Elizabeth a glare before her cheeks colored and she said, "My apologies. You saved my—"

Lydia!" How were they to keep last night's excursion a secret if Lydia spilled her guts at the first opportunity?

"Ernest. You did save Ernest."

"The seal?" Mrs. Forster cocked her head.

Elizabeth turned her attention back to Mr. Darcy, who, to her surprise, watched the interchange with the corners of his mouth pulling upwards.

Elizabeth said, "If you wish to sit, we can have tea or coffee brought for you." Her palms sweated, and an odd tingle ran through her chest and stomach as she gazed at Mr. Darcy. She had been too distraught the previous night to take much note of the lean beauty of his form, his chest and abdomen glistening in the falling rain as he stood, speaking to Mr. Dunham. Elizabeth had thought of it later, under her covers while Lydia slept.

Without him, Elizabeth and Lydia would have drowned. Elizabeth gestured towards an empty chair she had asked a servant to bring earlier that morning, hopeful Mr. Darcy would keep his promise and call on her.

Mrs. Forster rang for a servant who left and came back a few minutes later with a tray with tea and an assortment of fruit tarts.

Waving to a chair in the corner near the pianoforte, Mrs. Forster said, "Mrs. Anderson, if you will attend to our guests for a moment, Lydia and I need to retrieve a bonnet from my rooms."

Lydia cocked her head, and her mouth opened, likely to protest, but she shut it and nodded. "Yes. Mrs. Anderson will chaperone."

Mrs. Anderson, a stout, round faced woman with wide blue eyes and a brown, circular beauty mark on her right cheek, curtsied and sat. Within a minute, Mrs. Anderson was making a show of straightening up the area around the pianoforte while Elizabeth and Mr. Darcy sat together and stared at their plates.

Elizabeth ventured, "I apologize. This is most improper."

"Nonsense."

Elizabeth lowered her voice. "We might wish to

keep conversation to the weather and other such inanities," Elizabeth said, glancing at the door where her sister and Mrs. Forster were certainly listening.

Mr. Darcy spooned sugar into his tea.

"Three spoonfuls," Elizabeth said, charmed. "I am once again mistaken. I had not thought you fond of sweets."

"I am very fond, should the sweets be something to my taste."

Elizabeth's cheeks warmed. "Yes. I too am fond of sweets, when they are to my taste."

Elizabeth prided herself on making clever retorts, but her mind was a whirl of longing and fear with a touch of mortification. She asked, "Last night aside, are you fond of the sea?"

"I am."

"Is that where you learned to swim so well?"

"My father's valet taught Georgiana and I as children. Wickham as well, though he never lost his fear of the water. It was one of the few areas where I bested him. We took lessons together. He learned most things easily." Darcy's voice trailed off. He took a sip of his tea. "Though perhaps Wickham was far more adept at charming our instructors than mastering his studies." Mr. Darcy shook his head. "I apologize. I did not come here to discuss Mr. Wickham."

"He likely stole your notes while you were sleeping," Elizabeth said. "I am glad you warned me of him."

"Do you think he stole them?"

Elizabeth took a tart and held it between her fingers. "Considering his other crimes, stealing notes and pretending the knowledge was his own was merely a training practice."

Mr. Darcy smiled, and Elizabeth wanted to kiss him.

"You are very loyal," Mr. Darcy said.

"To those I care for." There. Elizabeth had made herself plain. What did it take to tempt a gentleman to kiss her? Mr. John Marley was her only experience, and he had taken the initiative in persuading her.

"Miss Elizabeth, I do not intend to be too forward, but a wise young woman mentioned recently that sometimes the most improper thing is the right thing to do. In some occasions."

"I remember hearing such a thing just yesterday." Elizabeth held out her hand. It was improper, as a guest in Mrs. Forster's home she did not wear gloves. Darcy took it, and they turn towards each other, fingers brushing.

"If it pleases you, I should like to call on you again. With the intention of paying court."

Elizabeth nodded. She glanced over her shoulder towards Mrs. Anderson at the piano, who, in the most improper motion, had turned her back to the two young people and dusted the shelves with a fervent focus.

Elizabeth leaned closer, her chin raised. "I should like that, very much."

Their lips met, soft and warm, and the tingle of desire ignited. Mr. Darcy cupped her chin, and her lips parted to meet his tongue. The chair rocked as she leaned closer.

Mr. Darcy brushed his thumb over her cheek.

The creak of a door opening. Mrs. Anderson called out, "Mrs. Forster. Miss Lydia."

Elizabeth and Darcy jerked back from each other. The chair tapped the floor as Elizabeth righted herself.

Lydia and Mrs. Forster came in, arms linked, giggling. Elizabeth's face flamed. How much had they seen?

Lydia said, "Is this not the loveliest bonnet?" She

held a straw bonnet, trimmed in lavender with a band of lace. "Mrs. Forster says I may borrow it for our seaside walk. And I suppose you two have news for us.

"Soon," Elizabeth said. She still held Mr. Darcy's hand.

Mr. Darcy said, "Soon."

And Jane was coming. She and Bingley would be reunited, and all would be well.

Lydia said, "You will join us for dinner tonight, Mr. Darcy?"

"We cannot ask him!" Elizabeth snapped. It was all well and good to be improper, but some standards needed maintaining.

Mrs. Forster said, "I will have my husband send an invitation. If you are free."

"It would be my pleasure," Mr. Darcy said.

# CHAPTER 24

**M**r. Darcy did not dine with the Forsters and Bennets that evening, but the following, to allow Mrs. Forster time to have a meal prepared for what became a large party: Bingley and Miss Bennet, Darcy and Elizabeth, Mr. and Mrs. Forster, Miss Lydia, Mr. and Mrs. Hurst, and Miss Bingley.

The latter focused on her meal, eschewing conversation about all but the most trivial topics. No one mentioned Mr. Dunham, but Mrs. Hurst sat close to her sister even as her husband—arrived in Brighton just that morning—plied Mr. Forster with tales of pheasant hunting and fine London dining, the latter a passion both shared.

Before the militia commander could discharge

him, Wickham resigned his commission, and, shortly thereafter, fled the country.

It should have upset Darcy for Mr. Wickham to once again escape justice, but he was too happy with Miss Elizabeth to much care. They walked together on the beach, Miss Lydia and Mrs. Forster serving as chaperone, many steps behind.

Miss Lydia returned to flirting, but her mishap on Mr. Dunham's sailboat had taught her some restraint. She did not run off on her own in the night, at least.

Bingley was deliriously happy, sending an assortment of brightly colored flowers to Miss Jane Bennet every morning.

Darcy knew his Elizabeth preferred the flowers imagination brought forth by the printed word far more than buds in truth and sent her a book every third day.

Elizabeth read them all, and they talked of them, and their lives. He told her of Pemberley, and of quiet places she would enjoy discovering on their walks, and the large pond where he had, as a child, practiced swimming. She told him humorous stories of her sisters and parents, and they held hands and exchanged a second kiss, after sneaking off from an assembly.

Miss Bingley made one attempt at recapturing Darcy's interest, but it was halfhearted at best.

Bingley, who had forgiven Darcy within a few days, said, "Caroline had me write to Mr. Dunham, and she affixed a missive on the bottom she would not let me read."

"And you agreed to this?"

"Either I agreed, or she would write him in secret." Bingley shrugged. "It is upsetting Mr. Dunham had to leave so quickly, considering the business with his father. They are both going to the Americas, I hear."

Darcy had not told his friend of what had transpired that evening, though the growing closeness between Darcy and Miss Elizabeth did not escape Bingley's notice. "If you propose to her a second time, be certain she accepts," Bingley advised.

Now, with only two evenings left before Elizabeth and her sister returned to Longbourn, Darcy's palms sweated as he paid call to Miss Elizabeth in the breakfast nook.

Elizabeth stood alone by the open window, the sun bathing her face and shoulders as she turned to him. She was alone.

Darcy bowed.

"My sister and Mrs. Forster will return in a few moments," she said.

Elizabeth glanced at the closed door on the opposite side of the room and put her fingers to her lips. They were listening in. Eavesdropping was a common habit in Miss Elizabeth's family, as she had revealed to him on more than one occasion.

"I understand," Darcy said. His mouth was dry, and he sweated.

Mr. Darcy, are you well?" Elizabeth took a step towards him.

"Very well," he said.

Elizabeth smiled. "Jane and Mr. Bingley are to be married at Christmas," she said. Her eyes shone. "I do not believe I have ever seen Jane so happy!"

Darcy smiled back at his love. Since Bingley had forgiven him, he plied Darcy with constant romantic advice. "Give her more flowers. And sweets. Ladies love sweets! Is Miss Elizabeth fond of gardening? Jane is." After announcing their proposal, Bingley used Jane's given name at every opportunity. "Jane," he would say, with the same reverence one gave poetry or a prayer. "How can a single sound possess such sweetness? A rose by any other name would be, always, Jane."

Darcy wondered if he should have brought

flowers and a box of sweets. He did not wish to make a hash of things a second time. He said, "About your sister's wedding..."

"Yes?" Elizabeth brushed her palm over her dress. She was nervous too. It gave Darcy the courage to plow ahead. "I remember you said you and your sister had always wished to have a double wedding."

Elizabeth laughed, a strained sound. "Some childhood wishes, I suppose, we must leave in childhood," Elizabeth said.

"Not all of them." Darcy took her hands. "If you would accept a second proposal?"

Elizabeth squeezed his hands. "I am open to a *certain* second proposal."

"Will you marry me, with your sister and my closest friend at Pemberley?"

"Yes. All of it. Yes!"

Darcy pulled Elizabeth, his Elizabeth, close and they kissed. She smelled of lavender and promise, her body tight to his, and he lost himself in her touch.

The door creaked open, and, "Lizzy! Mrs. Anderson was walking this morning, and she saw Ernest was on the shore, and he—! Oh!"

Elizabeth turned away for long enough to say,

"Lydia, Mr. Darcy and I are engaged."

"I should hope so! Else I have done a poor job ensuring your virtue, Lizzy!" Lydia giggled.

Elizabeth colored, and Darcy, not giving one whit about propriety, kissed her again.

## The End.

I hope you enjoyed reading this book as much as I loved writing it! If so, you can read more about the other books in the Jane Austen Challenge (they are awesome!) at JaneAustenChallenge.Com!

And learn more about my books, read free chapters, and get email updates at violetkingauthor.com.

Lastly, if you enjoyed this book and have a 3-minutes to leave a quick review, I cannot thank you enough! Reviews are how readers decide if they are ready to give a new author a try. For indie authors like me, having readers share their honest views about my books with other readers is a precious gift.

Thank you again so much for reading!

All the best,

Violet

## AUTHOR'S NOTE –ERNEST & REGENCY SWIMMING

I f you take a close look at the cover of Mr. Darcy's Seaside Adventure, you'll find Ernest the seal there, waving back at you.

The seal stemmed from a misunderstanding between me and Elizabeth Ann West. We were discussing our ideas for covers, and I said, "I want to have a watercolor beach scene and an old-timey seal on the cover!"

To which she responded, "That's a terrible idea."

A day later, she presents a red seal and says, "I had this wonderful idea!"

It turns out, when I said seal, she thought I meant a live, swimming in the ocean seal. This stemmed any number of jokes about seals with monocles, and in the end, we decided to put TWO seals on our covers, and try, if possible, to slip a seal into the content of our books somewhere.

Thus, Ernest was born.

Also, if you missed the introduction and want to learn more about swimming in the Regency Era (note: often in the nude), here's a great blog post which includes etchings from the time of nude lady swimmers. Or, as they said at the time, sea bathers.

Link: https://kathleenbaldwin.com/ladies-swim-regency-era/

# AN UNSUITABLE GOVERNESS

**S**parks fly when Miss Elizabeth Bennet takes work as a governess at Pemberley.

*Will deceptions, highwaymen, and a rambunctious eleven-year-old girl bring Elizabeth and Mr. Darcy together or tear them apart?*

After rejecting Mr. Collins proposal, Miss Elizabeth Bennet assumes the persona of a widow and goes to Lambton to find work. But when she befriends Mr. Darcy's half-sister Rose and becomes her governess, she must contend with Mr. Darcy, a man she wishes to despise, and Col. Richard Fitzwilliam, a man she wants to love but cannot.

With Rose's help, will Elizabeth find the strength to follow her heart?

Mr. Fitzwilliam Darcy would sooner face bandits than return to Pemberley and deal with his stepmother -- alas, he must do both. And when he discovers Miss Elizabeth Bennet in his home, serving as governess to his half-sister Rose, things go from bad to worse. Col. Fitzwilliam is falling for her. Mr. Darcy is too -- or would be, if Miss Elizabeth were at all suitable. Will Mr. Darcy stop denying his heart my before his cousin steals Elizabeth's?

Find out in **An Unsuitable Governess**, a standalone Pride and Prejudice novel of 64,000 words.

Warning! This book contains: one not at all wicked stepmother, one 100% wicked band of high-waymen, one rambunctious eleven-year-old, one deceptive governess with a heart of gold, one love-stricken colonel, one handsome gentleman in denial of his true feelings, one found treasure, and two happily ever afters to set your heart aflutter.

# CHAPTER 1

Beneath a gray and weeping sky, a Royal Mail stagecoach trundled north towards Derbyshire. Miss Elizabeth Bennet wished to pretend it was all a grand adventure, but three days being jounced about until her muscles and teeth ached and three nights in tiny coaching inn rooms with the thin, ill-tempered maid Mrs. Gardiner had insisted Elizabeth bring as a chaperone, had robbed Elizabeth of her sense of wonder. Her eyelids were stiff, her hair itched, and she stank.

Across from Elizabeth sat a white-haired, plump woman with spectacles on her nose and a book in her lap. She traced the text with her index finger as she read, pausing occasionally to take a sip from her hip flask or glance out the window at the patchwork fields.

Elizabeth glanced over at her, and then, fearing rudeness, turned her attention back to the pillow on her lap. Gripping the needle between her thumb and forefinger, she sewed. Beside her on the bench, the maid turned chaperone, Adelaide, slept with her head tipped back, mouth parted and snoring like an angry cricket.

"Is it your first time in a public coach?" the woman across from her asked.

Was it so obvious? Elizabeth stabbed the needle into the pillow. "Yes."

"It is not so terrible." The woman closed her book and placed it on the bench beside her. She lifted her hip flask and took a sip. "Have you and your... friend," she glanced at Adelaide. "Come up all the way from London?"

Elizabeth nodded.

"Long journey. You must be exhausted." The woman held out her hip flask. "Have a taste. It will warm your bones."

Elizabeth hesitated. She was not in the habit of accepting refreshments from strangers. "What is it?"

"My special mix for long trips. Go on, then."

Elizabeth glanced over at Adelaide, but the

maid did not stir. A fine protector. But Elizabeth was thirsty, and she appreciated the offer of friendship. She took the flask and sipped cautiously.

Liquid fire burned down her throat. Elizabeth coughed, blinking rapidly.

The old woman chuckled. "My specialty. Tea with a touch of lavender and a healthy dollop of gin."

"It is bracing," Elizabeth said, handing the flask back. Now that the initial burn had passed, the drink had warmed her, or at least distracted her from the chill, damp air and Elizabeth's own nerves.

"Are you visiting family up north?"

"In Lambton. And I am hoping to find work as a governess or a lady's companion."

Elizabeth's hands shook. She was really doing this, putting her life and her prospects behind her and seeking work.

After rejecting Mr. Collins' proposal, life at Longbourn had become intolerable. If her aunt and uncle had not visited and yielded to Elizabeth's entreaties to take her with them to Town, she might have buckled, not to Mr. Collins, who had already wed Charlotte, but to another fool with a good income whom Elizabeth did not admire.

No, it was better she left. The life of a governess

was uncertain, and for many unhappy, but if Elizabeth could not marry for love, she would not marry at all. And if she was not to marry, then she needed to provide for herself. She refused to be a burden to her family.

"Lambton! Why, that is my destination. My niece is with child, and I wished to give her some aid, what with her husband being away with Wellington's men. Have you any brothers on the front? We might pray, together."

Elizabeth was touched. "I have no brothers, but if you wish to pray..." Elizabeth had prayed enough this past month for guidance or at least comfort. Perhaps God had guided her here.

"In a bit, perhaps. You are not so fond of embroidery, are you, Miss—?"

Elizabeth bit the inside of her cheek. As tired and sore as she was from the days of travel, once she left this coach, her future became even more uncertain. "Elizabeth," she said.

The maid snorted and rubbed her hand over her cheek. Drool glistened from the corner of her mouth.

"Elizabeth Ben—" No. Once she left this coach, Miss Elizabeth Bennet would disappear. Best to begin now.

"Mrs. Elizabeth Wilson," Elizabeth declared. Wilson was her aunt's maiden name and the one she had chosen to begin her new life.

The old woman's eyebrow twitched. "Mrs. Wilson," she said, smiling with one missing tooth. "Evelyn. Mrs. Evelyn Johnson. It is a pleasure to meet you."

The carriage jerked.

"Huh?" Adelaide rubbed her eyes. The carriage jerked again. Elizabeth gripped the seat as ahead, the driver, astride one of the heavy draft horses, pulled back on the reins, shouting. The horses turned left, slowing beside a carriage which appeared to have tipped onto its side. The horses were gone.

"Goodness! I had not believed the rumors!" Mrs. Johnson exclaimed.

"Rumors?"

"Highwaymen."

Elizabeth swallowed. She peered out the side window. A footman hopped down from the coach. He held a coach gun in hand as he approached the downed carriage.

Adelaide said, "Cor! Mrs. Gardiner said no such thing of us being robbed."

"Perhaps there was an accident," Elizabeth suggested.

"Humph! What accident run off with the horses?"

Adelaide made an excellent point.

The footman returned, shaking his head as he walked back. He spoke briefly to the driver and then walked towards the back of the coach. Elizabeth stood.

"What are you doing?" Adelaide said as Elizabeth opened the stagecoach door.

"Finding out what is going on," Elizabeth said. A cold wind swept into the carriage. "Excuse me," Elizabeth shouted to the footman as he passed. "What happened?"

"Nothing to concern yourself with, Miss."

"Was anyone hurt?"

"No. It is empty."

An empty carriage, no horses, and rumors of highwaymen. Elizabeth shivered.

"We'll be on our way again, Miss, if you would like to get settled in."

Elizabeth thanked him and pulled the door shut.

"Cor," Adelaide said again as the coach

rumbled forward. "They gon' report it at the next station?"

"I suppose," Elizabeth said, seating herself again on the bench. As the driver guided the horses, Elizabeth reached up to the shawl around her shoulders and clasped it around her.

Mrs. Johnson took another swig from her flask. "Lambton is a quiet town. You were looking for work as a governess, you said?"

Elizabeth nodded. Thoughts of the empty carriage had driven away fears about her future employment.

"Try the Darcy house," Mrs. Johnson advised, holding the flask out again.

"Darcy?" It could not be the same odious Darcy who had mocked her and then danced with her with all the warmth of a plasterwork. Though Jane, or perhaps their mother, had mentioned Mr. Darcy's estate was in the North.

"At Pemberley. The youngest Darcy girl has been quite the terror since their father's passing, my niece says. She is just eleven and since last summer has driven away three young governesses on her own."

Pemberley. That was the name of Mr. Darcy's estate. Elizabeth had little doubt Mr. Darcy's sister was a terror. She would be following in the family tradition.

"Thank you," Elizabeth said, resolving to find work elsewhere. Highwaymen. Monster children, and now this.

"I would not have suggested it, love, but you were so fierce just then with the footman." Mrs. Johnson held the flask out again, and Elizabeth took it. Mrs. Elizabeth Wilson needed a taste of courage.

# ABOUT THE AUTHOR

Violet King is a Pennsylvania native who loves reading and writing Regency romance. She had some Pride and Prejudice plot bunnies that wouldn't leave her be, so she started writing her first JAFF in 2018. Her first book, Mr. Darcy's Cipher, is inspired by her interest in history and the desire to write about a smart, savvy heroine who saves her country while falling in love.

Violet's other interests include drawing and painting, trying specialty teas (she lived in Japan for a few years and is especially picky about Jasmines and Greens,) cuddling her cats, karaoke, and reading, reading, reading! You can learn more about her books and sign up for her newsletter at violetkingauthor.com.

Made in the USA
Monee, IL
15 February 2020